J
GUT

Gutman, Dan.

The million dollar
goal.

CHILDREN'S ROOM

$15.99

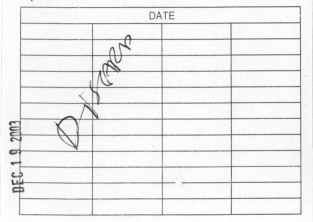

DATE			

DEC 1 9 2003

THE MILLION DOLLAR GOAL

THE MILLION DOLLAR GOAL

Dan Gutman

HYPERION BOOKS FOR CHILDREN
New York

First Edition

This book is set in 12/19 Palatino.

1 3 5 7 9 10 8 6 4 2

Printed in the United States of America

Library of Congress Cataloging-in-Publication Data on file.

ISBN 0-7868-1883-2

Visit www.hyperionchildrensbooks.com

To Donna Bray

Contents

A LITTLE LESS CONVERSATION

DAWN: You tell the story, Dusk.

DUSK: I'm not telling the story. I hate telling stories. And besides, I don't have time. I've got to go to hockey practice.

DAWN: Oh, come on. You've got more time than I do.

DUSK: Do not. I won't tell it.

DAWN: You're still mad. That's why you don't want to tell the story.

DUSK: I am not. That has nothing to do with it. I just don't want to. Look, you're the better writer. You're the one who gets straight A's every term. You like to read and stuff. You actually like doing homework! Just tell the story and leave me out of it.

DAWN: Well, it's true that I'm the better writer. But I'm the better hockey player too.

DUSK: Yeah, in your dreams you're the better hockey player! Man, why couldn't I have had a normal sister like other kids? Why did I have to have a twin?

DAWN: I feel the exact same way. Why couldn't I have had a normal brother?

DUSK: I guess it's a twin thing.

DAWN: What is?

DUSK: Feeling the exact same way. A lot of times you and I feel the exact same way. It's a twin thing.

DAWN: Yeah, but a lot of times you and I feel completely different. Look, how are we going to decide who's going to tell the story?

DUSK: I don't know. Rock paper scissors?

DAWN: No. You always cheat.

DUSK: Draw straws?

DAWN: No. Maybe we should flip a coin.

DUSK: Fine. Whatever.

DAWN: Heads, you tell the story. Tails, I tell the story.

DUSK: Flip it.

DAWN: Okay, here goes. . . .

DAWN: Okay, okay. I'll tell the story.

DUSK: And you'd better tell it exactly the way it happened.

DAWN: And what exactly do you mean by that?

DUSK: You always add stuff and change stuff around to make things sound better. This is my story too, and I want it told right.

DAWN: I do not "add stuff." What I do is called "descriptive writing." Just like Mrs. McElroy told us in Language Arts. And if you want the story told a certain way, why don't you just tell it yourself? That's what I said you should do in the first place.

DUSK: I'm not writing it. But I think I should get to read it every step of the way. And if there's anything I don't like, I should be able to change it.

DAWN: You will not change my words!

DUSK: I'm not going to let you screw everything up.

DAWN: I will not screw everything up!

DUSK: Well, I want some input.

DAWN: How about this. I'll write the story, and you

can read it. You can't change it, but you can add stuff if you feel I made any mistakes or left anything out. Like a footnote. How's that?

DUSK: Hmmm . . .

DAWN: Well?

DUSK: I'm thinking.

DAWN: That's a first.

DUSK: Shut up. Okay, that sounds all right to me. You write the story, and I get to add my own intelligent comments whenever I like. Deal?

DAWN: Deal.

DUSK: Good. I gotta go to practice. Just tell the story the way it happened.

DAWN: Okay, okay, here goes. I guess you can say it all started on the moon. . . .

PLAYIN' FOR KEEPS

"Ladies and gentlemen, welcome to LHL 3000. Tonight, it will be the visiting Lunar Hockey League champions, Kepler Tides, facing off against the home team, Tranquility Base Lunatics. Folks, it's a lovely night at Armstrong Stadium in the Sea of Tranquility. There's very little solar wind and the temperature is a nippy minus two-twenty-three degrees Fahrenheit, so the fans are bundled up. I guess we won't have to worry about the ice melting tonight—eh, Boomer?"

"Ha-ha-ha, that's right, Rick. We're just about ready to get underway. Both teams are gathering at center ice. Tonight's game is brought to you by the fine folks at Polar Spring Water. When your throat is parched and there's no moisture within a quarter of a million miles, nothing quenches your thirst like a Polar Spring."

"Boomer, they're facing off now. The referee has dropped the puck and it's floating slowly down to the ice. Legroin gets the puck over to Fisher. Fisher passes to Rockville in his own zone and he moves past the blue line. It's amazing how fast he can skate in lunar gravity while wearing that clunky spacesuit. I notice that Morris, the left wing for the Tides, is tugging at his mask."

"I noticed that too, Rick. He wants to make sure oxygen is flowing freely through the tubes. The slightest hole or gap and he would be dead in a matter of seconds. Jones is open on the right side. He is smacking his stick against the ice to let Rockville know he wants the puck."

"But wait, Boomer! Marshall checks Jones hard off the boards. He sails about ten feet over the ice. He's floating down now. Oh, his mask has been knocked off! He's gasping for air."

"It looks like he's dead, Rick."

"Yes, he is very much dead. Too bad. Kids, if you're playing in an airless environment, keep your mask on at all times. Tough break for the

Lunatics, Boomer. Jones is the second defenseman they've lost this week."

"It's all part of the game, Rick. Hockey is a rough sport, especially up here on the moon. At least he died almost instantly."

"Yes, we can be thankful for that, Boomer. There was no break in the action. The rookie, Robinson, is skating onto the ice as Jones's lifeless body is being carried off."

"Wait, Rick! Kempa of the Tides and Marshall have dropped their gloves. Kempa apparently thought Marshall made an illegal hit on Jones. The fists are flying now. These two are going at it! Oh, you hate to see that."

"I can understand getting a bit emotional after a teammate has suffocated in the first period, Boomer. But still—"

"Marshall is stomping on Kempa's stomach with his skate. Oh, that's got to hurt, even in one-sixth gravity! And now the fans are throwing moon rocks onto the ice. While the refs clear the ice, let's look at the fast-mo replay of Jones before he died."

"Well, it looked like a legal hit to me, Boomer. As play resumes, Fisher gets the puck just past the blue line. He's got an open shot and he slaps it over the goal, over the glass. . . ."

"That one's floating over the wall, Rick. It's going . . . going . . . it's . . . out of here! That baby might make a complete lunar orbit! Some lucky fan gets a souvenir, eventually."

"Will you please turn off that stupid video game!" Dad shouted from upstairs.

Oh, man. Our dad is so cliché. LHL 3000 is our favorite game. Playing hockey on the moon is really cool, and you can also customize the settings of the game so you can simulate the gravity, environment, and atmosphere of other planets in the solar system too.

Yeah, Dawn wants to play hockey on Uranus.

Oh, shut up, Dusk. Is that your idea of one of those intelligent comments you have to put in? You are so immature. I mean, does that really add to the story?

I couldn't resist.

Are you finished?

No.

Anyway, our dad doesn't exactly like hockey. He hardly ever comes to our hockey games, and

8

when he does come, he reads the newspaper instead of watching us play.

This is mind-boggling to me. How can anyone not like hockey? I mean, we live right outside Montreal! The first organized hockey game was played right here between two teams of students at McGill University back in 1875 at Victoria Skating Rink. You could look it up.

Hockey is our national sport. Canadians live and breathe hockey. Not liking hockey is just about against the law. Canadians not liking hockey is like the English not liking tea. Mexicans not liking tacos. Chinese people not liking . . . Chinese food.

Okay, we get the idea. But you know the real reason why Dad doesn't like hockey. He's not from Canada.

Well, that's true, I suppose. Our dad grew up in the United States, and baseball is his game. He would buy us bats and balls and gloves, but never any hockey gear. We have to buy that with our own money.

Now, baseball is a game I just don't understand. You've got nine guys pretty much standing around spitting and scratching themselves for a few hours. What's so interesting about that? Every hour or so, somebody will make a big hit or run or something, and then you have to sit around waiting another hour for something exciting to happen again.

I totally agree.

It must be a twin thing.

Meanwhile all those obsessed fans sit there arguing over whether the pitcher should have thrown a fastball or the hitter should have bunted or the manager should have picked his nose or whatever. Who cares? Give me some hockey action any day!

Dad took us to a few baseball games when we were little, hoping to turn us into fans. I remember he would lean over to me and Dusk and say something like, "Kids, the count is three and one, and there's a runner on first with one out. Do you think they should put on the hit-and-run to stay out of the double play?" And we'd say, like, "Whatever" or "Can I get ice cream now?" or "When is the game over?" He'd get so mad!

Remember the time we spent the whole game trying to get our faces on TV?

Yeah, that was great. If the truth be told, baseball is a wimpy game.

No argument there.

Now, hockey, *that* is a game! It's got everything. It's got speed. It's got excitement. It's got action. It's got skill and teamwork.

Oh, come off it. The best part about hockey is the fights. When two guys drop their gloves and start slugging each other, that is exciting! Did you ever see baseball players fight? They dance around like trained bears in the circus. It is pathetic. But nothing is cooler than watching two hockey players pummel each other until one of them has to be carried off the ice.

My brother is sick and needs counseling, needless to say. Hockey fights are fine for Neanderthals such as Dusk and his friends. I prefer to focus on the beauty of the sport. Did you ever watch a good hockey team bring the puck down the ice, passing smoothly back and forth? It is like poetry in motion.

As a matter of fact, last year in Language Arts Mrs. McElroy asked us to write a haiku about anything we wanted, and I wrote this one about hockey. . . .

> *Thin blades of steel glide,*
> *graceful in a frozen world.*
> *She shoots. She scores. Goal!*

I got an A for that. Mrs. McElroy told us that Japanese haiku is a way to capture moments of being alive by using sensory images. In writing them, you can express your personal spiritual philosophy and experience the feelings of the moment. In Japan, they're valued for lightness, simplicity, openness, and depth.

Wait a minute. I thought we had a deal that there would be none of your stupid poems in this story.

We made no such deal.

So we didn't make the deal, but you admit your poems are stupid?

I do not!

Oh, so your poems are stupid, but you aren't willing to admit it?

Will you shut up? My poems are not stupid. Look, you forced me to tell the story because you didn't want to. So please go play in the traffic or something.

Okay, but if you're going to put your stupid hockey haiku into the story, then you have to put my infinitely superior haiku in too. . . .

> *Bloody goon busts heads—*
> *Go to the penalty box!*
> *Get the puck out of here!*

You're an idiot, you know that? "Get the puck out of here" has six syllables, and a haiku always has three lines of five, seven, and five syllables.

Oh, what are you going to do, call the haiku police on me? What difference does it make?

Anyway, before I was so rudely interrupted by my obnoxious twin brother, I was trying to explain why hockey is the best game in the world. It is also one of the oldest sports. Most people don't know this. The first skates were made from animal bones. The game got its name from the stick, which was called "hockey" after the Old French word for the curved stick that shepherds used to carry: *hoquet*.

Can you wake me up when you're finished? Nobody cares about that boring history stuff. I'd rather watch a baseball game than listen to the history of hockey. Get on with the story.

Okay, okay. Dusk and I have both been playing hockey since we were little. First we were in the mighty mite league. That's for kids six years old and under. Then we moved up to the mite league, which is for seven- to nine-year-old kids. We were on the same team back then.

Now we're in the squirt league, where the boys

and girls play on separate teams. We're eleven, but when Dusk turns twelve and I turn thirteen, we'll move up to the peewee league. Most people who have seen us play agree that Dusk is the better skater, but I'm the better shooter.

Ahem. Excuse me? That's a lie and you know it.

He's probably right. I'm a better skater *and* a better shooter.

Shut up.

2

HARDHEADED WOMAN

The first thing that happened when we got home from practice (I scored two goals, by the way) was that our mom said she had good news for us. Dad got tickets to see the Montreal Canadiens play that night!

Well, we both just about fainted! Dad hardly ever takes us to hockey games. The tickets are expensive and hard to get, and after all, he doesn't even particularly like the game.

Dad told us he got free tickets for the whole family from one of his clients who had season tickets and couldn't use them that night. Dad works for an advertising agency and every once in a while he gets free stuff. But usually it's stuff we don't want, like coffee mugs and key chains.

As usual, Dawn has it all wrong. The first thing that happened when we got home that night was that Oma farted.

Do you have to write that? My brother is so disgusting!

Well, it's true. Oma is our grandmother. Her real name is Sophie Rosenberg, but we've always called her Oma. She farts all the time. If you're going to tell a story, you might as well tell it accurately. Remember what Mrs. McElroy said. Descriptive writing. You're supposed to paint a word picture and all that.

You want me to paint a word picture of Oma farting?

Yes!

Okay, well let me see if I can put this delicately. Oma lives with us. She's been living with us for years, ever since Poppop died. When she was younger, Oma and Poppop ran a little upholstery shop. They would fix people's couches and chairs and so forth. But she's been retired for a long time.

Oma is not in the best of health. That's another reason why she lives with us. She doesn't get around very well anymore. She uses a walker most of the time, and when she has to travel long distances she has to use a wheelchair, even though she doesn't want to. And yes, she has some problem with her guts or something that causes her to, uh, pass gas quite a bit.

It's called farting. It's not a dirty word. It's a perfectly natural bodily function. It cleans out the pipes. That's what Oma says. She says that's why she's lived so long. Because she farts so much that her pipes are really clean.

Okay, okay, farting. Fart fart fart. Are you happy now, Mr. Potty Mouth? We came home from practice and Oma farted. I was all grossed out, of course.

"What's the matter?" Oma said. "Haven't you ever heard a bleeping fart before? People bleeping fart! It's part of bleeping life. You might as well get used to it, because when you get to be my age, you'll bleeping fart all the time, that is, if you live this long."

Oh, I forgot to mention, that's another embarrassing thing about Oma. She curses a lot. Me, I don't curse at all. Some people might let out a curse word when they stub their toe, or if they hit their thumb with a hammer. But to Oma, cursing is like one of the parts of speech or some-thing. Nouns, verbs, adjectives, and four-letter words.

Mom and Dad tried to get her to tone it down, especially in front of me and Dusk, but it was no use. She's old and set in her ways.

"Freedom of speech includes cussing," Oma always says.

So Dusk and I were all excited about going to the hockey game that night, but Oma didn't want to go. She never wants to go anywhere. That's why we hardly ever get to go on family vacations. And when we do go, sometimes we have to come back early because Oma says she wants to go home.

Anyway, Oma started in with her usual when-I-was-your-age routine.

"When I was your age," she said, "we didn't go to bleeping hockey games. We did our bleeping homework at night. We did our bleeping chores. What chores do you kids have? None. That's why you'll never amount to anything. All you do is play bleeping hockey and those bleeping video games. You never worked a day in your bleeping lives."

Don't forget Velvet Elvis.

Oh yeah. Oma is in love with Elvis Presley. Apparently she met him when she was younger, and ever since then all she cares about is Elvis. Elvis Elvis Elvis. The guy has been dead for, like, eternity, but Oma still worships him.

"He's still alive, you know," she always says.

Yeah, right. Oma is one of those people who thinks Elvis faked his own death and he's still running around out there somewhere. Every so often you hear that somebody spotted Elvis shopping at Wal-Mart or ordering a burrito at Taco Bell. Oma is one of those people. I'm sure she would see Elvis all the time if she ever went outside.

She's got this Elvis shrine in her room, and she insisted that Mom and Dad put up this big framed portrait of Elvis over the couch on the living-room wall. Mom says the picture is "khalooscious," which I think means "horribly ugly" in Yiddish. I'm sure I didn't spell it right, but I know it starts out with that clearing-out-your-throat sound.

It's on velvet!

Yes, and that makes it even more repulsive. We call it Velvet Elvis. A couple of years ago Dad took Velvet Elvis off the wall, thinking Oma might not notice. But the second she came into the living

19

room, she just about threw a fit and Dad had to put Velvet Elvis back.

Oma says that Elvis Presley himself gave her Velvet Elvis as a present, and that it is her good-luck charm. So we have to keep it up on the wall until Oma dies, I suppose.

The point I was trying to make is that Oma is a bit of an embarrassment to us all. Dusk and I never have friends over to our house. Oma is always home. We know she's going to curse and say rude things and fart in front of our friends. And we know our friends would go back to school and tell everybody we've got this giant Elvis on velvet hanging on the living-room wall. They would think we were a bunch of freaks.

Why don't you come out and say it?

Say what?

Say what we talked about.

I'm not going to say that!

Then I will. We both agreed that we kinda sorta ~~wished Oma would die already~~.

Dusk, that's a horrible thing to say! I'm crossing that out.

Go ahead, but it's the truth.

3

MONEY HONEY

None of us thought anything of it when we saw the sign outside the Molson Centre that said MIL-LION DOLLAR GOAL CONTEST TONIGHT. At least none of us said anything about it at the time. I figured it was probably a charity promotion that the players would be participating in, or something like that.

The only thing Dusk and I were thinking about was the game. We hadn't seen the Canadiens for about a year (except on TV, of course) and we were really looking forward to seeing them play. They're our hometown team, and we're big fans.

Dusk and I are too young to have seen the Montreal greats from the past—Maurice Richard, Guy Lafleur, Dickie Moore, and the rest—but I've seen pictures and film of them. The Canadiens have won twenty-four Stanley Cup titles since the team started way back in 1909. They're probably the best team in the history of professional hockey.

The Molson Centre is right in the middle of downtown Montreal, just west of Windsor Station. As we pulled into the parking lot, Dusk was already bugging Dad to tell him where our seats were. Dusk likes to sit behind the goal so he can watch the goalie. I'd rather sit in the middle so I can follow the flow of action.

Dad pulled out the tickets while he was getting Oma's wheelchair out of the trunk.

"Section two-oh-three, row L, seats one through five," he said.

"Oh, man, section two-oh-three sucks, Dad!" Dusk complained. "You can't see squat from there."

"The seats were free," Dad grumbled.

"We don't have to stay, Dusk," Mom said sweetly. "If those seats aren't good enough for you, you can stay home and do nothing."

Mom has a way of putting things into perspective. Dusk shut his mouth.

"Why do I have to sit in that bleeping

wheelchair?" Oma said in the parking lot. "I'm not a bleeping cripple."

Even though we were able to park in a handicapped spot, it was still quite a distance from the stadium, and Oma would not have been able to walk it.

"I just want you to be safe, Mom," Dad said. He was having a hard time unfolding the wheelchair. I could tell from the tone of his voice that he was tired of hearing complaints. After all, he was taking us all out to a hockey game, and he doesn't even like hockey.

I went over to help him with the chair. It took a long time to transfer Oma out of the car and into the wheelchair. Dad's video camera was hanging around his neck, and every time he moved, the camera would bang into the wheelchair or the car.

Dad is a video nut. He has one of these tiny little video cameras and he takes it everywhere. He tapes everything. He has a huge collection of videos down in the basement.

"Someday, all this will be yours," he likes to say about his tapes. Dad is so cliché. I'd hate to break the news to him that everything is on DVD now and his collection of tapes is obsolete.

"Why did we have to bring Oma?" I overheard Dusk whisper to Mom. "She couldn't care less about hockey."

Dusk knew perfectly well why we had to bring Oma. It wouldn't have been safe to leave her home by herself. If she had fallen down, she might not be able to get up. There might be an emergency if she was home alone. She might not be able to get to a phone. I mean, we leave her home for an hour or so if we have to, but not often. I think Dusk was just impatient to get inside and watch the Canadiens warm up.

Excuse me if I correct the facts here for a moment. It wasn't that I didn't want Oma to come to the game with us. It was just that I thought she would be happier staying at home. She doesn't like hockey, and she would be able to watch TV.

Yeah, right. Nice try, Dusk. Anyway, we finally got Oma into the chair and made our way into the Molson Centre. It was still early, but the place was already filling up. The Canadiens usually sell out. Mom got me cotton candy and Dusk some popcorn. I made sure to thank her, and Dad too, for getting the tickets.

We took the elevator to the 200 level so

we wouldn't have to push Oma's wheelchair up the ramp. Mom and Dad had to struggle with it after we found section 203. The rows were just a few inches wider than the wheelchair, and it kept bumping the seats on the sides. Then they had to pick Oma up and transfer her to the regular seat. And she was complaining the whole time.

"I can't bleeping see," Oma said once she was finally settled in her seat. It was true. Oma is really short. There was a guy in front of her, and his head was blocking her view.

"What does she need to see for?" Dusk whispered to me. "She'll probably sleep through the whole game anyway."

"Dusk, you switch seats with Oma," Dad said.

"Oh, man!"

It took another five minutes or so for us to pick up Oma and switch her over to the next seat. By the time we were finished, warm-up was over and the game was about to begin.

"Don't forget, fans!" the announcer said. "Stick around at the end of the game. That's when we will select the winner of our million dollar goal contest."

A buzz went through the crowd. A guy in the row behind us said that they were going to pick one fan to take a shot, and if he made it, he would win a million dollars.

"Or she," I told the guy. "It could be a girl, you know. Girls play hockey too." The guy just rolled his eyes.

Dusk claimed he could put a puck in the goal from anywhere on the ice with his eyes closed. He probably could. The only problem was that the Molson Centre holds more than twenty thousand people. So each of us had a one in twenty thousand chance of getting picked to shoot the million dollar goal.

"Very clever marketing," Dad said. "By having the contest at the end of the game, they are making sure nobody leaves early."

"What difference does it make if people leave early?" I asked. "They already paid for their tickets."

"Well," Dad explained, "if people stick around until the end, they'll buy more food, more drinks, more souvenirs, spend more money. Hockey teams probably generate more revenue from concessions than they do from tickets."

I had never thought about that. But I guess marketing and stuff is Dad's business, so he thinks about it all the time.

As it turned out, a lot of people left early anyway. The Canadiens had a bad night, and the game was a blowout. They were behind 4–0 after the first period, and it just kept getting worse. I had never seen them so flat. There weren't even any good fights to hold Dusk's interest. Oma was asleep in her seat by the second period, and none of us bothered waking her up. Dad was shooting video, for no apparent reason.

"Let's get out of here," said Dusk, who hates to see the Canadiens get clobbered.

"It would be nice to beat the traffic out of the parking lot," agreed Dad, turning off his video camera.

"Oh, come on," I said. "We only get to see one hockey game all season. Can't we stay till the end?"

"Okay," Dad grumbled.

At the end of the third period, the Canadiens' coach had pulled out all the regulars and replaced them with a bunch of new guys none of us had ever heard of. The final score was something like

8–1. Some of the fans were booing as the players left the ice.

"Okay, hockey fans," the public-address announcer suddenly boomed, "who wants to win a million bucks?"

Everybody screamed, and we stopped thinking—at least for a while—about how terribly the Canadiens had played. The house lights went on, and a couple of guys started wheeling something out to center ice. I looked through Dad's binoculars and could see it was a big TV camera on a rolling tripod.

"Tonight, we are going to pick *ONE* lucky fan to take *ONE* shot on goal. And if that *ONE* lucky fan is lucky enough to hit the target, that *ONE* lucky fan will win . . . *ONE* . . . million . . . dollars!"

"Yeeeeaaaaahhhhhhhhhhhh!" the crowd roared.

Dad pulled out our tickets to look at the numbers on them. I had heard about these contests before. They have them in basketball, football, baseball, and some other sports too. They usually pick one ticket randomly and the person holding that ticket gets to shoot, kick, or throw something at a target to win a lot of money. It's never easy, and the person almost always misses. The pressure must be incredible, with all those people watching you.

"You can put your tickets away," the public-address announcer said. "Ladies and gentlemen, we've got another way to find our lucky fan. . . ."

The big JumboTron screen at the far end of the rink lit up. You could tell that it was hooked up to the TV camera that was at center ice, because the camera was slowly rotating around in a circle and the image on the JumboTron was spinning. The camera was sweeping across the crowd.

"Very clever," Dad said. "They realize that the younger generation of hockey fans responds to pictures better than words. These guys know their business."

As the camera swept by our section, Dusk and I got up and waved. So did everybody else. I thought I caught a glimpse of us up on the JumboTron, but it went by so fast I wasn't sure.

"Fans, as you know, this was the last game of the current homestand. But the Canadiens will be back after a long road trip. Tonight, we will select our lucky fan. And one month from today, on February twenty-first, that lucky fan will be invited back here to the Molson Centre to shoot for that million dollar goal."

"Brilliant," Dad said. "They're trying to sustain interest in the team during the road trip and pump up the attendance for the next homestand. I'll bet the Canadiens will be playing the weakest team in the league on February twenty-first. Now they'll sell out that night instead of having thousands of empty seats. Brilliant marketing. No wonder these guys can afford to give away a million dollars."

"Do you think we have a chance to win?" Dusk asked me as the camera panned past our section.

"Sure we've got a chance," I said. "A one in twenty thousand chance."

"Around and around and around she goes," the annoucer said. "Where she stops, nobody knows."

A wave had spread across the crowd. As the camera rotated, all the fans in the section it was pointing to stood up and screamed.

"I'm getting dizzy just looking at that," Mom said. "I wish they would pick somebody and get it over with."

"They're trying to heighten the drama," Dad explained.

"Will you be in the lucky section?" the announcer asked. "Which lucky section will it be?"

The camera stopped spinning suddenly. It was pointing in our direction.

"Section two-oh-three!" the announcer hollered.

Everybody in our section screamed. I could see our faces, even though they were very tiny, up on the JumboTron. People in the other sections booed, and many of them started heading for the exits.

"Hey, maybe it's good we didn't leave early," Dad said. He turned on his video camera again and started shooting.

"Do you think we have a chance now?" Dusk asked me.

"Maybe one in a hundred," I replied, looking around to estimate how many people were sitting in section 203. "Or one in two hundred."

The TV camera didn't rotate anymore. Instead, it started to zoom in and out. So the image on the JumboTron showed a single row when it zoomed in, and then when it zoomed out, it showed all of section 203.

"In and out and in she goes," the announcer said. "Where she stops, nobody knows!"

"That man is really annoying," Mom said. "I wish he would be quiet."

"Will you be in the lucky row?" the announcer asked. "Which lucky row will it be?"

The camera stopped zooming suddenly. It was pointing at our row.

"Row L!"

Everybody in our row screamed. I could see our whole family up there on the screen, along with some other people on either side of us.

"Do you think we have a chance *now*?" Dusk asked.

"About one in fifteen!" I said, trying to hold back my excitement. But it wasn't easy. My heart was racing. I couldn't stay in my seat. I might be the lucky one!

The camera started to bounce back and forth, left and right, like it was following a tennis match. It was moving faster now, so I could hardly see myself as it panned past my face.

"Now it's time for us to find the lucky seat!" the announcer shouted. Everybody was screaming, even Mom and Dad.

"Let it be me. Let it be me. Let it be me." Dusk had his eyes closed, his hands clasped, praying.

"Back and forth and back she goes," the announcer said. "Where she stops, nobody knows!"

They must have had a drum machine or something, because a drumroll was pounding out of the speakers. People were clapping along with it and stomping their feet.

"Will you be sitting in the lucky seat?" the announcer asked. "Which lucky seat will it be?"

"Please please please please please please," Dusk mumbled.

And suddenly, the camera stopped. One face filled the JumboTron screen.

It was Oma. She was fast asleep.

THAT'S ALL RIGHT, MAMA

For a moment, we all just sat there, stunned. There was dead silence in the Molson Centre.

They *couldn't* have picked Oma! Out of all of us in Row L, out of all the people in section 203, out of all the fans in the whole stadium, they had to pick a little old gray-haired lady who could barely walk?

Mom and Dad gasped. I heard the people sitting at the end of our row sighing and moaning that they never win anything. Dusk pounded his armrest.

I was pissed! I wanted it to be me so badly! I could make that shot easily. And I was sitting in the lucky seat! If Oma and I hadn't switched seats before the game began, it would have been *me* that was picked to shoot the million dollar goal. It wasn't fair.

Oma opened her eyes and let out a fart.

"Can we go home now?" she asked. "I have to go to the bathroom."

Some of the fans were laughing as they gathered up their coats and things and headed for the exits. A representative for the Canadiens ran over and handed us some paperwork to take home with us and sign.

None of us were sure if Oma even knew what had just happened to her. She had been asleep most of the game. Oma sometimes has trouble sleeping at night, so we hadn't bothered waking her.

When they showed her image on the JumboTron, her eyes were closed. Maybe she slept through the whole thing. Maybe she didn't even know she had been selected to shoot the million dollar goal. Maybe it would be best if she didn't find out.

I looked at Mom and Dad. Dad put a finger to his lips to let me and Dusk know we should keep our mouths shut.

Nobody said anything in the car on the way

home. It was really awkward. This incredibly amazing thing had happened and we were all bursting to talk about it, but nobody was saying a word. We just kept shooting looks at one another. It wasn't until we got home and put Oma to bed that me and Dusk and our parents gathered in the living room to talk it over.

"I know what you're all thinking," Dad said to open the discussion. "But Oma is not going to take that shot."

"That's not what I was thinking," Mom said.

"Oh, man, why not, Dad?" Dusk complained. "What if she makes it? It's a million bucks!"

"She's not going to make it," Dad said. "Don't be ridiculous. She's an eighty-year-old woman who uses a walker."

"She might fall down and break her hip," Mom pointed out.

"The whole experience would be humiliating for her," Dad said. "That's my decision. I'm not going to change my mind."

I told Dad he was crazy. A million bucks is a lot of dough. He could buy a lot of stuff with a million bucks. A new car, one of those cool new video systems, anything he wanted.

"I'm not going to humiliate my mother so I can get a cool new video system."

Dusk said he would. It looked like a family war was going to break out. I wasn't sure who was right or which side I should take. But I tried to think of a solution that might make everybody happy. Or at least make everybody not so mad.

"Maybe," I suggested, "they'll make the shot easier for Oma in some way. They can't expect an old lady who can barely walk to be able to shoot a puck like a young person with no handicap could, right? Why don't we talk it over with the Canadiens? They're good people. Maybe we should find out all the details before we decide whether or not she will try it."

I agreed with Dawn (for once). Must be the twin thing. Dad was assuming that Oma would have to take a regular shot. But people with physical handicaps get to use ramps instead of climbing steps, right? They get the best parking spaces so they don't have to walk far, right? Maybe the Canadiens would make some accommodation for Oma. Like maybe she would get to shoot from the crease instead of the blue line. Something like that.

"You know what I think?" Dad said. "I think

they chose Oma on purpose because she is an old lady who can't walk. They probably spotted us coming into the stadium with the wheelchair and decided right then that they would pick her of all the thousands of people in the stands."

"Why would they do that?" I asked.

"So they wouldn't have to pay out a million dollars, of course!" Dad explained. "They knew that if they picked a cripple, it would be impossible for her to make the shot. She probably wouldn't even take the shot in the first place because her family cares about her and wouldn't let her. Oh, these people are marketing geniuses. They know all the angles."

The discussion would have continued, but at that moment Oma came rolling into the living room in her wheelchair. She had her nightgown on. We all looked up, surprised. I had thought she was in bed for the night.

"Anybody see my bleeping teeth?" she asked. "I can't find 'em anywhere."

Oma is always losing her false teeth.

"Did you look in your mouth, Oma?" Mom asked.

Oma reached into her mouth and pulled out her

teeth. "Oh, yeah. I forgot to look there. Bleep. Good night."

Mom rolled her eyes. It was not the first time Oma had lost her teeth in her mouth. She turned around to roll back to her bedroom.

"Oh, by the way," she said, looking back at us. "I'm not a cripple. And I'm going to take the shot."

5

DON'T BE CRUEL

"Any way you slice it, Pirelli Pizza is the nicest," Dad said as we ate breakfast the next morning. "What do you think of that?"

"I hate it," Dusk said, grabbing his third pancake.

"Don't you get it?" Dad said. "Slice of pizza? Any way you slice it? That's a great slogan for a pizza place."

"I get it, Dad," Dusk countered. "It's dumb. And 'slice it' doesn't rhyme with 'nicest.' How about this—Pirelli is smelly?"

"Very creative, Dusk," Mom said, getting a cup of coffee. "Short and sweet."

"Smelly?" Dad said, wrinkling up his nose.

"One of the cardinal rules of advertising is, never use the word *smelly*."

"Not all smells are bad smells, Dad," I pointed out. "Pizza is supposed to smell. People love the smell of a good pizza."

"*Smelly* is an ugly word," Dad insisted. "You wouldn't even use *smelly* if you were creating an ad for perfume."

Dad's advertising agency had recently landed the Pirelli Pizza account, and we were trying to come up with a new slogan for them. They didn't like their old slogan—"A little bit of heaven in your mouth." That's probably why they had switched advertising agencies. We spend a lot of time in our house trying to dream up slogans.

We batted around a bunch of ideas until Mom finally broke in and asked, "Has anybody thought about what we are we going to do with Oma? She's going to wake up and come in here any minute."

"What were the exact words she said before she went to bed last night?" Dad asked.

"She said, 'I'm going to take the shot,'" I recalled.

"Maybe she was hallucinating," Dusk said.

"Maybe she was talking in her sleep," suggested Dad. "She does that sometimes, you know. Maybe she won't even remember what she said, or what happened last night."

"It's possible that we misunderstood her," I pointed out. "You know, like when you hear a song and you get the words wrong?"

Mom once told us that when she was a girl, she had heard this song by a guy named Bob Dylan, where he sang, "The answer, my friend, is blowing in the wind," but Mom thought he was singing, "The ants are my friends blowing in the wind." I always thought it was funny.

"Yeah," I said. "Maybe she didn't say 'I'm going to take the shot' at all. Maybe she said, 'I'm going to take you shopping.'"

"Maybe she said, 'I'm going to take a crap,'" Dusk said.

"Language check, Dusk!" Mom warned.

"Hey, Oma is the one who said it, not me."

"Look, it doesn't really matter what she said last night," Dad said. "What matters is what we're going to say when she comes in here for breakfast this morning."

"Maybe we shouldn't say anything," I suggested. "Maybe we should just play it cool and see what she says."

Everybody agreed that was probably the best way to go. We would see if she brought up the million dollar goal herself.

A few minutes later, Oma came hobbling into the kitchen behind her walker. She was singing one of those old Elvis songs she loves so much. I'm not sure which one it was, but one of the lines was, "Wop-bop-a-loom-a-boom-bam-boom." Can you believe people used to listen to that music? I slid over so she could get into her seat more easily.

"Where's the bleeping newspaper?" Oma asked, grabbing a pancake. "And where are my bleeping scissors?"

"Must you use that language in front of the children?" Mom said.

"You mean English?" Oma asked. "Oh bleep, they hear those bleeping words in the school yard every day."

"Well, they don't have to hear them in our kitchen too," Mom said.

I gave Oma the Sunday paper and she started

going through it. Oma doesn't actually read the paper. She couldn't care less about the news of the world. She doesn't cut out coupons, either. The only reason she wants the paper at all is for the contests.

Oma loves contests. She enters the Publishers Clearinghouse Sweepstakes every year. She buys lottery tickets. She enters contests that are on the backs of cereal boxes and cake mixes. We have to buy foods that none of us even like because Oma saw on a TV commercial that there was a contest she could enter.

Every Sunday there are usually four or five contests in the paper, and she enters them all. She'll enter contests to win dumb things like a bag of sponges. She'll enter contests to win things she couldn't possibly use, like sports cars, boats, and even Super Bowl tickets!

It drives Dad crazy. I guess it's because he's in the marketing business and he knows the odds of winning any of those contests are a zillion to one.

"If you still had all the money you've spent entering contests," he likes to tell Oma, "you'd be a millionaire today."

But Oma doesn't care. She spends hours going through these entry forms carefully, making sure she places each little sticker where it is supposed to be, each card in the proper envelope, filling in each blank exactly how it is supposed to be filled in, and making sure she gets her entry form in the mail before the deadline.

"You've got to play by the bleeping rules," Oma always tells us. "If you don't play by the bleeping rules, you can't bleeping win."

Of course, Oma never won anything. That is, she had never won anything until last night.

It was looking like Oma had forgotten all about the million dollar goal contest. She hadn't said anything about it, and the rest of us were all being careful not to mention it. And then Dusk had to go and say—

Now, wait a minute! All I did was ask Oma if she'd had a dream the night before. Don't blame everything on me.

"Yes, I did have a dream last night," Oma replied.

We all shot hopeful glances at each other. Maybe Oma thought that the whole Million Dollar Goal contest had been a dream.

"I dreamed my bleeping teeth fell out," she said. "So I went into the living room to look for them, and you were all in there talking about how Oma the dumb old fart probably was asleep at the hockey game last night and wouldn't remember anything."

"Nobody called you a dumb old fart, Mom," Dad said.

"So you were awake the whole time, Oma?" Mom asked.

"Of course I was bleeping awake! When I'm dead, I'll be able to sleep for the rest of my life. I had my eyes closed because I was praying! It's about time it paid off."

"So you're really going to shoot for the million dollar goal, Oma?" Dusk asked.

"You're bleeping right I am. I've got enough bleeping life in me to push a bleeping coaster into a bleeping net. And then I'll be dancing in the end zone when they hand me that check for a million big ones, believe you me."

"Oma," Dusk said, "it's not a coaster. It's called a puck. And they don't have end zones in hockey. You must be thinking of football."

46

"Football, hockey, who the bleep cares?" Oma said. "Gimme another pancake."

I looked over at Dad. He was shaking his head slowly from side to side. I could almost hear his brain trying to come up with an argument he could use to talk her out of shooting for the goal.

"Mom, it's really not a good idea," he finally said. "You're just going to embarrass yourself in front of a lot of people."

"You think I'm embarrassed because I've got no bleeping teeth?" Oma asked him.

"No."

"You think I'm embarrassed because I can't bleeping walk like a normal person?"

"No."

"You think I'm embarrassed because I bleeping fart a hundred times a day?"

"No."

"Well, I'm not going to be embarrassed by this, either," Oma said. "The truth is, you're the one who is embarrassed by me."

"I am not," Dad insisted.

"Don't worry," Oma told him. "Soon I'll be dead and I won't be able to embarrass you anymore."

"Mom!"

Boy, and I thought Dusk and I had a hard time getting along with our parents! Dad and Oma were really going at it. I suppose everybody fights with their parents about silly things, no matter how old we are.

"You kids don't know this," Oma said, "but I was quite the athlete when I was a young girl."

She tossed that off very casually, but it took me a little by surprise. It was hard to imagine Oma being a young girl, much less an athlete. She hardly ever mentioned her childhood or told us stories about growing up. Whenever anybody asked her about her childhood, she would just say it wasn't very interesting.

It occurred to me that I hardly knew anything about my grandmother except that she was an old cranky lady. I guess I just assumed that she had always been an old cranky lady, even as a girl. Now it seemed like she was letting us in on a little secret.

"What was your sport, Oma?" I asked.

"I won the Hungarian junior ladies' pole vaulting championship one year," Oma said proudly.

"How many Hungarian junior lady pole vaulters were there?" Dusk asked.

"None of your bleeping business!" Oma said. "There would have been a lot more, but they knew they couldn't beat me, so they didn't try."

"Mom," Dad said. "I'm sure you were a great pole vaulter in your day. But that was sixty years ago. You could get seriously hurt if you tried to do something athletic now."

"What's left to hurt?" Oma said. "When I get up in the morning, everything hurts. When I go to bed at night, everything hurts. Pain doesn't hurt anymore. It's just part of life. I'm a bleeping adult. I make my own bleeping decisions. I won the bleeping contest, I'm going to take the bleeping shot, make the bleeping goal, and win the bleeping cash. And you can't stop me."

With that, Oma threw the newspapers on the floor.

"Kids, I think you should go upstairs," Mom said. "This is adult conversation."

There was no way I was going anywhere, I'll tell you that much. Things were just getting interesting. Dad was really getting hot under the collar. I wanted to stay and watch the fireworks.

"You know," Dad said to Oma, "all these contests you enter are no way to get rich. Contests are just marketing gimmicks that companies put on to sell products, or increase their market share, or create mailing lists. The only way to get rich is by doing long, hard, honest work."

"I worked hard all my life," Oma said. "Where did it get me? You have no right to tell me about honest work. You're a bleeping advertising man! It's your job to tell lies that will convince dumb saps to buy pizzas and pimple creams they don't need. You call that honest work?"

"There's no talking to you," Dad said. "Go ahead and take the shot if you want to. It's your life."

"Fine," Oma said.

At that point, it was like all the air had been let out of a balloon. Mom started clearing the dishes off the table. Dad stomped off to go read one of his detective novels, which is what he does in his spare time. I told Mom that Dusk and I had to go to hockey practice.

"Not so fast, you two!" Oma said as we were about to leave.

"Yes, Oma?"

"First you've got a chore to do."

Dusk and I looked at each other.

"Uh, we don't have any chores, Oma," Dusk said. "Remember? You always complain that we don't have chores."

"You do now," she replied. "You're going to teach me how to play hockey."

6

TREAT ME NICE

There's this pond by the woods behind our house—

I would just like to go on record as saying that Dawn is doing an excellent job of relating this story pretty much the way it happened so far. That's why I haven't interrupted very much.

Thank you.

Also, from now on, when my name comes up in the story, I would like you to refer to me as "The Rocket."

What?!

I want you to call me Rocket. Dusk "The Rocket" Rosenberg.

Why?

That's my nickname.

Since when?

Since right now. I just thought of it. I've always hated my name. The only reason Mom named us Dawn and Dusk was because that was how long she spent in labor with us. I always wanted to have a nickname. The great Rod Gilbert of the Canadiens was called "The Rocket." I like the sound of that and I want to be called "Rocket" too. Why, can you think of a better nickname?

How about Dusk "The Dork" Rosenberg?

Go ahead and laugh. Someday, thousands of hockey fans will be on their feet chanting "Rocket! Rocket! Rocket!" You'll see.

Okay, "Rocket" it is. If I may continue, there's a pond behind our house. It's back almost by the woods. It's not very big, about the size of a hockey rink. We fish in it during the summer, then it freezes up most of January and February unless we have a really warm winter. I often wonder what happens to the fish when the pond ices over.

They die. That's what happens to them.

Dusk!

Rocket is the name. Hockey is the game.

Okay. "Rocket" and I learned how to skate on the pond. We must have been only four or five when Mom got us our first ice skates, the ones that have two runners. Rocket threw his away years ago, but I still have mine in my room on a bookcase with my other stuff to remind me of when I was little. They're so tiny, it's hard to believe I ever fit my feet into them.

These days Rocket and I usually skate at St-Michel, a rink near our house, because it's regulation size and the conditions are better for playing hockey. But every so often it's fun to go out on the pond. Nothing beats skating outdoors, with the wind in your face.

Uh-oh. I think I feel another haiku coming on.

Just ignore him. We thought the pond would be a good place to take Oma to practice, because it's pretty isolated and so close to our house. Still, it took about a half an hour to get her out there. Rocket had to lug the stick and the goal through the snow, and I had to lug Oma. She refused to use the wheelchair, so I had to help her with her walker to make sure she didn't fall down.

You know what I want to know? Why do they call it a walker? If you can walk, you don't need one. You only need a walker if you can't walk. So they should call it a can't-walker.

Are you finished?

No.

Just ignore my brother. We got Oma out to the center of the pond, and I was kind of frightened. I mean, Oma can barely walk on solid ground. Now she would have to walk on ice. Not only that, but she would have to hold a hockey stick in her hands and shoot a puck with it.

Rocket laced up his skates, and then he set up the goal at the other end of the pond, about fifty feet away. It's one of those goals made from plastic tubing that you fit together and weave the netting around the tubes. I didn't bring my skates. I thought it would be easier to help Oma if I was wearing sneakers. Rocket skated back over to Oma with the stick.

"Now, Oma," he began, "here's how you hold a hockey stick. You put your right hand here and—"

"Just give me the bleeping stick," Oma said. "What do you think I am, an idiot?"

Rocket handed her the stick and she grabbed it with her hands together, the way you would hold a baseball bat. She leaned on the walker with her forearms.

"Where's the bleeping coaster?" she demanded, waving the stick around.

Rocket took the puck out of his pocket and held it up for Oma to see. "Now the puck is made of hard rubber. The key thing about shooting it is—"

"Just put it down," Oma instructed.

Rocket dropped the puck on the ice in front of Oma without saying another word. She eyed it for a moment, and then she took a swing at it with the stick. It wasn't even close. The blade passed about a foot above the puck. The stick slipped out of her fingers and slid across the ice.

"That's not bad for a first try, Oma," Rocket said. "But the idea is to send the puck down the ice, not the stick."

"Don't get smart with me," Oma said. "Gimme that back."

Rocket skated over to retrieve the stick. He handed it to Oma. This time she put the blade right on the ice behind the puck. Then she gave the blade a little shove forward. It pushed the puck maybe five inches.

Rocket looked to me, and then we both began

clapping. "Yeah, Oma! Way to go!" we hollered. "Great shot!"

"Knock it off," Oma said. "It hardly went anywhere. I don't need your bleeping pity."

I put the puck back in front of the walker and Oma tried again. It was pretty much the same result. She had pretty good arm strength, but she didn't seem to understand how to get the blade on the puck. She kept trying, but the puck never went farther than a foot or so.

We tried to explain to Oma how to grip the stick correctly and how to shoot, but she just wouldn't listen. She only wanted to do it her way.

Oma *did* seem to understand that if she could get the stick moving faster, it would propel the puck farther. She began swinging at it again. Half the time she would hit it a few feet, and half the time she would miss completely.

"This has been a good practice," I said when it seemed like Oma was getting tired. "We'll try again tomorrow, okay?"

"One more shot," Oma said. Rocket put the puck down for her.

She gripped the walker with her left hand and took the stick in her right. She brought it back to about shoulder height, and then whipped it down with as much force as she could generate, which wasn't a whole lot.

The blade hit the ice about five inches in front of the puck, so she wasn't able to follow through on her shot. The stick slipped out of her right hand, and her left must have loosened its grip on the walker. Her feet must have slipped on the ice too, because the next thing we knew, Oma was off balance and spinning around backward.

I tried to grab her arm, but I was too late. She fell down, crashing heavily against the ice.

"Oma!" we both shouted, rushing to her.

The first thought that crossed my mind was that Oma was dead. She wasn't moving. It was my fault. I had killed my grandmother.

"Don't touch her!" Rocket warned. "If she's paralyzed or something, she shouldn't be moved!"

"I can't get up," Oma finally groaned. "I think I bleeping broke something."

I ran to get Mom and Dad while Rocket stayed with Oma. A few minutes after Mom called, an ambulance arrived. The paramedics brought a stretcher out to the pond and carefully lifted Oma onto it. I was relieved that she was alive, but I still felt terrible. I didn't know how badly she was hurt.

"It's really not such a good idea for a woman in your condition to be playing ice hockey, ma'am," one of them told her.

"Bleep you," Oma said. "You're not a doctor."

I held Oma's hand as they loaded her into the ambulance. I remember how dry and papery it was. But it was warm too.

We had to sit in the waiting room at the hospital while Oma was being X-rayed and examined. Finally the doctor came out. He introduced himself as Dr. Patel, and he said he had some good news and some bad news. We all braced ourselves.

"The good news is that nothing was broken," Dr. Patel said. "Mrs. Rosenberg is going to be just fine."

Dad let out a big sigh of relief. While we were waiting, he had told us that older people's bones aren't as flexible as ours and they can break very easily if they fall. They don't heal as easily, either. Sometimes elderly people even die if they break their hip.

"What's the bad news?" Mom said, looking worried.

"The bad news is that Mrs. Rosenberg is a terrible hockey player. She really has no chance of making the NHL if she's going to fall down taking a simple slap shot."

We all laughed, but I, for one, thought that was a lame joke. Why is it that doctors always have to tell you they have good news and bad news? And why is the bad news always some lame joke? What happens if there really *is* some bad news, like the patient has two weeks to live? Do they still tell you a lame joke? I'll bet doctors have to take a course in medical school to teach them how to tell good news and bad news jokes.

Are you finished?

No.

"Your grandmother is a feisty lady," Dr. Patel told us, smiling a little. "She refused to take any painkillers. She said that Elvis Presley took painkillers, and that's what killed him."

Oma was going to be okay, Dr. Patel told us. But he said he didn't want her to use a walker anymore. She wasn't stable enough. The time had come for her to switch to the wheelchair full time.

"At least she'll give up on this silly notion of

shooting a million dollar goal," Dad said as we went to see Oma in her room. "Some good will come out of this."

The first thing I noticed when I saw Oma lying in the hospital bed was that she looked so old. She didn't look like herself anymore. She looked tired. The doctor said she seemed feisty, but she didn't look very feisty to me. That fall had taken some of the fight out of her. I think we all noticed.

She looked like she was nearly dead, is what she looked like. I didn't think it was possible for somebody to look so different so quickly.

We gathered around her bed, making small talk for a while. She seemed happy to see us. I knew Dad was afraid to break the news about the wheelchair to Oma. She was sure to argue about it, and Dad hates arguing with her.

Finally it was Mom who brought up the subject. "Oma," she said gently. "The doctor said he doesn't want you using the walker anymore. He feels you should be in the wheelchair. It's for your own safety."

Oma turned her head to the side and sighed. "I know," she said quietly. "I guess I won't be dancing in the end zone after all."

Then she turned her head back to us.

"But I'm still going to take the shot."

We brought Oma home from the hospital that night and set her up in her room with some magazines, TV, stereo, and a stack of her favorite Elvis Presley records. The doctor had ordered her to rest in bed for two days with no physical activity at all.

That night, Rocket and I went into our parents' room for a talk. We had both agreed that if Oma insisted on shooting the million dollar goal, somebody else should coach her. We felt bad about what had happened the first time, and we were afraid she might get hurt again. Oma didn't listen to anything we told her to do anyway. And besides, we had our own hockey to think about.

Mom and Dad listened to what we had to say and said they understood how we felt. But they wanted us to continue coaching her anyway.

"Do you remember when your other grandmother died?" Mom asked.

"It was right after New Year's," Rocket said. "I remember that."

"That's right," Mom said. "When she got older, Grandma used to say she wanted to live to see the twenty-first century. She died on January third, 2000. She had achieved her goal, and then her mind and body quit."

"People need something to live for," Dad continued. "Something to look forward to. Mom and I have our careers and each other and watching you kids grow up. That's what we live for. You've got school and hockey and your friends and your future. That's what you live for. But what does Oma have to live for? Not much."

"These contests she's always entering give her something to get excited about," Mom said. "Even if she never wins any of them, they give her something to wake up the next morning for."

"But she can be . . . such a drag to be around," Rocket said.

"I know," Mom said, putting an arm around each of us. "You know how sometimes you like a person, but you don't love them?"

"Yeah."

"Well, I think the reverse is possible too," Mom said. "You can love a person and not particularly like them. We can love somebody because they are our cousin or our brother or our grandmother, and that's a good enough reason to love them."

"Look, Oma is eighty years old," Dad went on. "Someday she will pass away, and you won't have any grandparents anymore. I know she can be difficult to be with sometimes, but let's all try to love her anyway while she is still with us. And the way to show her you love her is to help her with this silly contest. Okay?"

"Okay."

7

THE WONDER OF YOU

Oma doesn't play DVDs, CDs, MP3s, or minidisks. She doesn't even play cassette tapes. Oma has an old record player that plays these big old black records called LPs. They actually use a little needle that rests on a groove in the record and the vibration of the needle against the groove creates the sound. Hard to believe, isn't it?

After a while, the needle kind of messes up the groove and the record sounds scratchy. Oma's records are about fifty years old, and they all sound pretty scratchy.

"Come here," she said to me the day after she came home from the hospital. "I want you to listen to something."

I knew it was Elvis Presley as soon as she

dropped the needle on the record. I could recognize the voice. Besides, Oma hardly ever played anything except Elvis. She played me a song called "Rip It Up," bobbing her head up and down slightly with the beat.

"What do you think of that?" she asked when the song was over.

"Cool," I lied.

"You're just trying to make me feel good," Oma said. "I can tell you hate it. But do you think that fifty years from now anybody will be listening to that rap noise you kids like so much? Bleep no. But Elvis, his music will live on after all of us are gone."

"Didn't people say the same thing about Elvis Presley fifty years ago, Oma?" I asked. "Didn't they say he was just a fad, and that his music was just noise?"

"I suppose they did." Oma sighed. "Ah, someday you'll appreciate Elvis."

She had me listen to another song. While it was playing, she closed her eyes and mouthed the words.

"I was thinking," she said when the record was done, "when I die, I want one of those Elvis impersonators to deliver my eulogy."

She was creeping me out. Old people talking about dying creep me out.

It occurred to me that she was giving up, just like my other grandmother gave up after she had lived to see the new century. Oma didn't ask for the newspaper to look for contests to enter. She didn't turn on the TV. Instead, she was listening to her old Elvis records and planning her own funeral.

I told Rocket I was worried, and we decided we weren't going to let it happen. We couldn't cure Oma's physical problems. We couldn't make her young again. But we could make her into the best hockey player she could possibly be.

It wasn't going to be easy, because she wasn't an easy student. We would have to be tough on her. We would have to take charge. And we wouldn't take any of her guff.

We took one of Rocket's old hockey sticks and sawed it down so it was only a few feet long. If you're sitting down, like in a wheelchair, you can generate a lot more power if you shoot with a short stick, holding it with just one hand.

We went over to the sporting-goods store and bought some plastic ice. It comes in eight-by-four-foot sheets and it's made of some stuff called ethylene polymer. It's not as slippery as real ice, but it lets you practice skating and shooting a puck when you can't get to a regular ice rink. Perfect for Oma.

We had Dad call up the Montreal Canadiens promotions department. I had noticed that the contract they had given us at the game didn't say anything about sitting down for the shot. We wanted to make sure it would be okay if Oma took her shot from her wheelchair using the short stick.

The lady on the phone was real interested in Oma, and she said it was fine for her to shoot from a sitting position. She also said she would send over a new contract specifying that the contestant would be in a wheelchair on the night of the big shot.

Finally, we were ready for Oma.

"Get out of bed!" we announced as we marched into Oma's room the next morning. "It's time for hockey practice and your coaches don't like to be kept waiting."

"B-but the doctor told me to rest another day," Oma protested.

Rocket put his face close to Oma's. "Would Elvis rest?" he asked. "Would bleeping Elvis sit around listening to old Elvis records when there was a bleeping million dollar goal to be shot?"

"Where did you learn such language?" Oma asked.

"From you. Now get out of bed."

Oma looked a little surprised at our new attitude, but for once she did as we told her. We transferred her to the wheelchair and rolled her out to the driveway. Rocket had put the goal out there, with the sheet of plastic ice just a few feet away. We had decided that it would be smarter to put the goal close to Oma at first. If she was able to score from a few feet, then we would gradually move the goal farther away. As our folks said, people always need to have something to aim for.

Rocket and I have a lot of experience with hockey sticks. You're supposed to put your dominant hand at the end of the stick, or just below the knob, if there is one. Your thumb goes behind the shaft and wraps around to meet the tip of the forefinger. If you put your thumb on the top of the shaft, your shot will be weaker. Basically, you want to shake hands with the stick.

It's really not that different if you were to hold the stick with one hand. We gave Oma the shortened stick and showed her how to hold it. Since the fall she had taken on the real ice, she seemed more willing to listen to what we had to say. She was more passive, more dependent on us now.

"There are five places to shoot," I told her. "Bottom left corner, bottom right corner, top left corner, top right corner, and between the goalie's legs."

"How about I shoot it right down the middle?" Oma asked.

"Good plan," Rocket said. "There won't be a goalie. Now, there are five kinds of shots you can take. The wrist shot, snap shot, flip shot, slap shot, and backhand shot. The slap shot looks the coolest, because it's the fastest and it makes a great noise when the puck hits the target. Some players can hit a slap shot a hundred miles per hour. But it is also the hardest shot to learn, and you look really stupid if you miss."

I suggested we teach Oma how to do a wrist shot, which is the easiest shot to make, and the most accurate too. Rocket agreed, and he showed Oma how to use her wrist and fingers to control the stick. You don't want to squeeze the shaft too hard, and you want to make sure to keep your elbow up so your wrist can roll as you shoot.

We showed her how to shoot with the puck in the middle of the blade or near the heel, where you have the most control and strength. When a shooter is standing, the legs and hips provide most of the power, but Oma would have to rely on a long sweeping arm motion and a follow-through toward the target.

"How come you kids know so much about this stuff?" Oma asked.

"Hockey is our Elvis," I explained.

Oma took the short stick in her hand and practiced the sweeping motion against the plastic ice. It was a lot easier for her than trying to use the long stick while holding on to the walker. And as long as she was sitting in the wheelchair, she couldn't fall down. She got the hang of it quickly. Her right arm was very strong, she told us, because of all the years she had spent sewing cushions and pillows and slipcovers.

Rocket put a puck down on the plastic ice and told Oma to try and hit it into the goal. Oma put the stick behind the puck and whipped her arm forward. The puck went right down the middle and into the net.

"She shoots!" we hollered, jumping up and down joyfully. "She scores!"

"Move me back," Oma instructed. "That was too bleeping easy."

We moved her back to ten feet or so and she took another shot, hitting the puck right down the middle again and into the net.

"Farther," she told us.

She put a few shots in from fifteen feet too, and we were really getting excited. Rocket jumped in front of the goal and pretended to be trying to stop the shots. Even Oma cracked a smile or two when we would yell and scream each time she put a puck into the goal.

I hadn't noticed, but some boys had gathered across the street to watch what we were doing.

"Hey, Rosenberg!" one of the boys hollered to Rocket. "When did you switch to the senior league?"

"Yeah," another one of them yelled. "It's about *time* you found somebody you could compete against!"

The boys across the street were laughing their heads off and pointing at us.

"Friends of yours?" Oma asked Rocket.

They were some jerks I'd seen around. I guess they played for one of the other teams in our league. I didn't even know their names. I felt like going over there and telling them to get lost, but there were three of them and one of me.

"Hey, you!" Oma shouted at the boys. "Come here!"

The kids looked at each other, then they came across the street and stood in front of Oma.

"Listen, you bleeping little bleeps!" she said, pointing her finger at each of them. "Why don't you mind your own bleeping business? You come around here again and I'll bleeping beat the bleep out of you! So bleep off!"

Then Oma let out a fart that would curl your teeth. The boys ran off like they'd just seen Godzilla.

"Too bad Oma can't shoot the puck with her mouth," I said.

Her mouth? Too bad she couldn't shoot it out of her butt. That million dollars would be a sure thing.

8

FOLLOW THAT DREAM

We worked with Oma every day that week. Some days she was into it, hitting the puck pretty straight and hard. Other days she was too tired or not feeling well and she wasn't any good at all. She wasn't anywhere near ready to take a shot from across the rink yet, but I'd say she was making progress.

On Friday, Dad came home from work with his car loaded down with big cardboard boxes. This was not unusual. He works with a lot of different clients and sometimes he has to carry around samples of whatever product it is they are selling.

"Where's Oma?" he asked, lugging in one of the boxes from the garage.

"She's napping," Mom said.

"Check this out," Dad said, cutting open the box with a razor blade.

He reached into the box and pulled out a bright yellow T-shirt. On the front of the shirt was a big photo of Oma's face. Above the face were the words THE MILLION DOLLAR GOAL and below it SOPHIE ROSENBERG. Then he flipped the shirt over and on the back were the words GO, GRANNY, GO!

"What do you think?" Dad asked us excitedly.

For a moment or two, we all just stood there. I didn't know what to say.

You know how some things are cool and some things are uncool? And some things are so cool that they're not cool anymore, like a song that gets played on the radio so much you can't stand it? And some other things are so uncool that they actually become cool, like the Weather Channel?

Well, I wasn't quite sure where these T-shirts fit in on the coolness scale. They certainly weren't cool, to my eyes. They may have been uncool. But they may have been so uncool that they were actually cool. That was Rocket's opinion.

"Awesome shirts, Dad!" he said. "Can I have one?"

Mom, on the other hand, clearly did not think the shirts were cool at all.

"Ugh," she said, holding her hands in front of her eyes as if the T-shirts were blinding her. "You put your own mother on a tacky T-shirt? Weren't you the one who said you didn't want her to humiliate herself? And the yellow is horrible."

"I think the yellow is cool," Rocket said.

"How many of these monstrosities did you print up?" Mom asked.

"Ten thousand," Dad replied. He explained that they cost just two dollars each to make, and he figured he could sell them for fifteen dollars each on the night Oma takes her shot. So if he makes thirteen dollars on each shirt and he sells all ten thousand of them, they would bring in $130,000.

"Not bad for a night's work," as Dad likes to say. He is so cliché.

Those numbers didn't impress Mom. She still thought the T-shirts were a bad idea. And if nobody wanted them, Dad would have spent $20,000 and ended up with nothing but a garage filled with useless T-shirts.

"Maybe you should think about having your mother's body cryogenically frozen," Mom suggested. "You could make a lot of money selling her DNA after she dies."

That is called sarcasm. Mrs. McElroy taught us about sarcasm in Language Arts. It's when you make fun of somebody by saying the opposite of what you mean.

Oh, thank you, Rocket, for adding that very crucial information.

That's sarcasm too. I am so-o-o-o-o glad that you appreciated my sarcastic comment. Hey, that's sarcasm too!

Are you finished?

No.

"Look," Dad said, "the kids have been working hard with Oma, but I think we all know that she's got about as much of a chance to make that shot as I do of winning the Nobel Prize. If you think she's going to come home that night with a check for a million dollars, you're dreaming. But if we sell these T-shirts, at least she'll get some money out of this."

I'm not one to go prying into my parents' finances. We're not rich. I know that because Mom and Dad are always trying to save a few dollars here and a few dollars there. But I don't think we're poor, either.

I do know that Oma's medical bills add up. Medications and doctors and wheelchairs and stuff cost a lot of money. Oma doesn't have much money of her own. That's one of the reasons she has been living with us all these years.

"Isn't there a more tasteful way to raise money?" Mom asked, but Dad couldn't think of one.

It didn't really matter what any of us thought about the T-shirts. The only opinion that counted was Oma's. A few minutes later, she came rolling into the kitchen.

Oma picked up one of the shirts and looked it over carefully, front and back. She stretched the shirt, held it up to the light, and sniffed it. It had been many years since she had worked as an upholsterer, but she still remembered what to look for in a fabric.

"I'll take ten," she said.

A couple of days later, Rocket and I were watching the local news on TV. They always save the sports report for the end, so you have to sit through half an hour of crime, traffic accidents, celebrity news, and corrupt politicians before they get to the good stuff.

"The Canadiens were off today," the announcer

said, "but we still have some hockey news for all you die-hard fans—"

And then, Oma's face appeared on the screen.

"Mom! Dad! Oma!" we screamed at the top of our lungs. "Come in here quick!"

Mom and Dad came racing into the living room like the house was on fire. Oma rolled in after them, complaining about all the noise and fuss.

On TV, somebody was interviewing Oma. She was sitting there on our couch wearing one of the yellow T-shirts with her own face on it. Velvet Elvis was on the wall behind her.

"They say hockey is a young man's game, but when the Canadiens return from their road trip on February twenty-first, Montreal's oldest female hockey player will be taking the ice at the Molson Centre after the game against the Chicago Black Hawks. Mrs. Sophie Rosenberg will have the opportunity to take one shot on goal. If she makes it, she will be one million dollars richer."

"You didn't tell us you had been interviewed for the news!" Dad said to Oma.

"Do I have to bleeping tell you everything?" she replied. "They came over yesterday while you were grocery shopping."

"Mrs. Rosenberg," the interviewer continued. "Do you really think you can put the puck in the net?"

"What the" *bleep* "kind of question is that?" Oma asked. "Of course I'm gonna put the" *bleep* "ing puck in the" *bleep* "ing net. You think that just because I'm an old bag I can't" *bleep* "ing shoot? Believe you me, after I score that" *bleep* "ing goal, I'll be dancing in the" *bleep* "ing end zone."

Then Oma farted. We could actually hear it on TV.

The interviewer looked all flustered. He didn't quite know what to make of Oma, or what he should do next.

"O-kay!" he finally said. "Dancing in the end zone! Well, uh . . . tell me, Mrs. Rosenberg, what's the story with this Elvis on the wall behind us. Is that velvet?"

"Don't touch the King!" Oma scolded the guy, slapping his hand away before it could reach the portrait. "Do I come over your house and touch your" *bleep* "ing stuff?"

Rocket and I cracked up. "Oma, you're famous!" Rocket said.

"I guess you told *him* a thing or two, Mom!" Dad said.

The interviewer tried to make a graceful get-away, but we didn't hear the ending of the report. There was a knock at the front door and the phone was ringing. Mom got the door. It was a kid who lived down the street. He wanted to know if he could get Oma's autograph. Dad got the phone. It was a newspaper reporter wanting to know if he could do a story on Oma.

As soon as Dad hung up, the phone rang again. And again. And again. Everybody we knew was calling to say they had seen Oma on TV. A lot of our friends didn't even know about Oma, because we never invited anybody over to our house.

"I just spoke with this complete stranger who asked me if he could order some of the T-shirts Oma was wearing on the news," Dad marveled as he took the phone off the hook to prevent it from ringing again. "Can you believe that?"

"How many did he want to order, Dad?" Rocket asked.

"A thousand," Dad replied, shaking his head. "I think I'd better print up more T-shirts."

DEVIL IN DISGUISE

We try to make sure somebody is home with Oma all the time. Dad has flexible hours, and Mom works at home most of the time. While Rocket is at hockey practice I'm usually at home, and he's home when I'm at practice, most days anyway.

I was home with her one day when a man came to the door.

"May I speak with your grandmother?" he asked politely, and when she rolled into the living room he added, "in private."

The guy didn't look like a mass murderer or anything. He was short, chunky, balding, well-dressed. He had a cigar in his mouth, but it wasn't lit. Lighting up would have been a big no-no in our house.

He said his name was Sheldon Silverman. He didn't look like he would do any harm. Oma is a grown-up, after all. It's not like I was her baby-sitter. I excused myself and went up to my room to listen to music.

After a while I came back down just to see if everything was okay. The Silverman guy was already gone. Oma was watching one of her soap operas on TV.

"Who was that guy," I asked Oma, "a sales-man?"

"No, he was a nice Jewish boy," she replied. "He gave me this. . . ."

When anybody tells Oma he is Jewish, she immediately likes him. A man is always "a nice Jewish boy"; a woman is always "a nice Jewish girl." This Silverman guy could have been a homo-cidal maniac. But if he was Jewish, he'd be "nice." Oma even insists that Elvis Presley was Jewish, but that's another story.

Oma handed me three or four sheets of paper that were stapled together. On the top of the first sheet, it said PROFESSIONAL SERVICES AGREEMENT. There were a bunch of paragraphs after that, but the print was really small and it didn't make a lot of sense to me. The final page had Silverman's signature at the end, and below that was Oma's signature.

It was obviously a contract of some sort. I've never signed any contracts, and I don't know much about them. But I do know that a contract is sort of like a promise, except that if you break the promise you could lose all your money or even go to jail.

I was concerned, because it didn't seem like a good idea to sign a contract with a stranger who just walked up to your door and talked with you for a half an hour.

I called Dad at his office and told him what happened. He was home a few minutes later, reading the contract even before taking his coat off. As he got deeper into it, his eyes started bugging out.

"Mom!" he yelled, "Tell me you didn't sign this. Please tell me this isn't your signature."

"Sure I signed it," Oma said. "I'm a big girl. I'll sign whatever bleeping thing I want to sign."

"That guy was an agent, Mom! You signed a contract for him to represent you for five years. Do you know what that means?"

"It means he's gonna make some bleeping money for me," Oma said. "Product endorsements, commercials, that sort of thing. He thinks he might even be able to turn this million dollar goal thing into a book or a movie. It could be a lot of bleeping cash."

I was afraid Dad's eyes were going to pop out as he read the small print on the contract.

"Do you realize," Dad said, trying to keep his voice steady, "that for every dollar this guy makes for you, he gets to keep sixty cents?"

"So if he makes a million bucks I get $400,000," Oma calculated. "That's $400,000 more than I have in my pocket right now. And I don't have to do a lick of work. I say it's a good deal."

"Mom, he can do *anything* with your name and picture! He can sell you like toothpaste. You really should have consulted me."

"Did you consult *me* when you printed those T-shirts?" Oma said, pointing a finger at Dad. He shrank back, defeated. "You think small, that's your problem. You want to hawk T-shirts from the trunk of your car. Silverman is talking Hollywood, the Internet, *The Tonight Show*. That's why I signed with Silverman. He thinks big."

Dad looked hurt. He couldn't help Oma get all those things Silverman promised. He hadn't even known she wanted those things. None of us did.

"I just wish you had waited, at least," Dad said quietly. "We could have looked over the contract together, evaluated it, negotiated with him . . ."

"There was no time," Oma explained. "He had to catch a plane. He's on his way to California right now to cut some deals for me."

We figured out pretty quickly that Silverman was a liar. Dad called Silverman's office in Montreal and his secretary said Silverman was too busy to talk. He would be tied up in meetings all day. So he had never gone to California. When Dad tried to schedule an appointment with him, he was told he would have to wait two weeks.

"That man is a sleazeball," Dad said after hanging up the phone.

My father has never been an assertive man. When we're in a restaurant and he doesn't like his food, he'll never send it back. He just eats it or leaves it. He says he doesn't want to make a fuss.

But Dad was really steamed about this Silverman thing. When Mom came home from work, he told her what happened, and they agreed that the only thing to do would be to go to Silverman's office personally and demand to see him.

Rocket was told to stay home with Oma, but Mom and Dad brought me along because I had seen Silverman in person. I would be able to identify him in case he tried to pretend he wasn't the same guy who had come over to our house.

The address on the contract was a high-rise building not far from the Molson Centre in downtown Montreal. When we got off the elevator on the twenty-eighth floor and entered the office of Silverman & Company, a bunch of phones were ringing and employees were hustling back and forth carrying paperwork.

The receptionist asked very sweetly who we were and if we had an appointment. When Mom said we didn't, the receptionist said it would be impossible to meet with Mr. Silverman today. But Dad wasn't having any of that.

"You tell your boss," he said, "if he refuses to meet with us, maybe the police will have the time to meet with us. I'll be calling my lawyer too."

A few minutes later, we were ushered into

Silverman's office. He was sitting behind a big desk, with a big, unlit cigar in his mouth. His copy of the contract with Oma was lying on the desk in front of him. I nodded to Dad to let him know that it was the same guy who had been over to our house. The walls were lined with photos of Silverman shaking hands with various celebrities.

"Mr. and Mrs. Rosenberg!" Silverman said, a big toothy smile on his face. "Shalom! It is so nice of you to shlep all the way over here. People don't stop by just to visit anymore. That's a *shandeh*, don't you think? May I offer you something to nosh on? A cup coffee?"

"You can drop that Jewish stuff," Dad said, looking coldly at Silverman. "The fact that you are Jewish and I am Jewish has no bearing on our discussion, Mr. Silverman."

I knew the Jewish expressions would make no impression on Dad. He hadn't been inside a synagogue since his bar mitzvah when he was thirteen.

"You are absolutely right," Silverman said. "Please, sit down."

"Mr. Silverman, I would like to make this as brief and as civil as possible. My mother is a very old woman, and she is not in the best of health."

"Those are precisely the qualities that make her an attractive spokeswoman, Mr. Rosenberg!" Silverman said, his eyes dancing with delight. "The moment I saw your mother on TV, I thought, she's honest, she's earthy, she's opinionated, she's real, she's got chutzpah—I mean, she's got nerve. She could be the voice of her generation!"

Silverman never took the cigar out of his mouth the whole time he was talking, but he never lit it, either. He just chomped on it the whole time. Finally I couldn't stand it anymore. I asked him why he didn't light the cigar.

"My doctor told me smoking is bad for me," he said.

Silverman told us that he had already begun cooking up book deals, movie deals, and television appearances for "Slap-Shot Sophie." That's what he called Oma. Slap-Shot Sophie.

A company that makes playing cards wanted to put her picture on a deck of Old Maid cards, Silverman said. There was interest in having her do commercials and magazine ads for constipation medication and diapers for adults who couldn't control their bowels. A television producer wanted to make Oma the star of a TV special called "Who Wants to Marry an Elderly Millionaire."

I was watching Dad's face while Silverman was describing the big plans he had for Oma. It went from tan to pink to red to purple.

"I can see it now," Silverman continued, spreading his hands up in the air as if he were looking at a picture. "There will be a Slap-Shot Sophie line of hockey sticks, of course. We'll sell millions of packs of Slap-Shot Sophie bubble gum. Slap-Shot Sophie bobble-head dolls! This million dollar goal is chicken feed, Mr. Rosenberg. It's only the beginning. The possibilities are unlimited. I'm going to make your mother a very wealthy woman!"

"NO . . . YOU . . . WON'T!" Dad said, getting up from the chair until he was towering over Silverman. "My mother will not be a part of this."

"Mr. Rosenberg, I have a signed, legally binding contract. Your mother is a grown woman—"

"My mother is a senile old lady who can't make these decisions for herself!" Dad hollered. "You can take your signed contract and . . . no, I'll do it myself."

Dad picked the contract up from Silverman's

desk and ripped it in half. Then he ripped it in quarters and threw the pieces in Silverman's face.

Man, I wish I could have been there to see that.

"You can't do that!" Silverman shouted as Dad motioned for me and Mom to go. "I've already done a lot of work on your mother's behalf, and I expect to be paid for it. I'll call the cops on you!"

"I'll call the cops on *you!*" Dad shouted back. "You should be arrested for taking advantage of helpless old ladies! You'll be hearing from my lawyer!"

Dad slammed Silverman's door so hard on the way out that I thought the glass was going to shatter.

When we were back in the elevator, Dad was breathing really heavily. He mopped the sweat off his forehead with a handkerchief. Mom and I hugged him all the way down to the lobby.

"Dad," I told him, "you were great!"

DON'T ASK ME WHY

There were two weeks to go before Oma would be shooting for the million dollar goal, and she was showing definite improvement with every practice session. She had learned that if she held the short stick the way Rocket and I told her to hold it, she could shoot better.

Leaning over the side of her wheelchair, she was beginning to swipe at the puck with a smooth and powerful motion. She was working hard to get better.

From the start, her shots were on target almost all the time. According to Oma, she was always good at "threading the needle."

Mom and Dad bought more sheets of plastic ice so Oma could practice her shots from farther away. We gradually moved her back to fifty feet, and she was reaching the goal about half the time. A lot of young people who *aren't* sitting in wheelchairs can't do that.

Our practice sessions were usually after school from four o'clock to five. Word must have gotten around, because people started showing up on the sidewalk in front of our house to watch. Oma was becoming the neighborhood celebrity.

Rocket and I hadn't spent this much time with Oma since—

Since we were born, really. Taking care of two babies was really hard on Mom, so Oma helped out. And after Mom went back to work, Oma took care of us pretty much by herself for a while. She was already starting to have trouble walking when we were babies.

Before this whole million dollar goal contest, Oma was just our cranky old grandmother who disapproved of everything we did. She probably thought of us as annoying kids who made too much noise and weren't respectful toward grownups.

But as we practiced every day, Oma was getting to know us a little better, and the other way around, too. Sometimes between shots she would ask us about what happened at school that day or she would tell us a little something about what life was like when she was growing up. She didn't yell at us as much as she did before her fall on the ice.

"Why are you doing this?" Rocket asked Oma at the end of one practice. Oma had been working really hard, and she looked exhausted. "Why are you putting yourself through this? You don't have to. You could be sitting home watching your soap operas."

A few people were on the sidewalk watching practice, so Oma rolled over to us so she could talk to us quietly.

"My parents were poor," she said. "They left me nothing when they died. Your grandfather and I came to this country with no money. All we had was the dream of making something of ourselves. Well, Poppop died young, I got sick, and now I'm just as poor as my parents were."

"It doesn't matter to us if you're rich or poor," I told her.

"Maybe not. But if I win this contest, I will have achieved something. I will have bettered myself.

That's human nature. We want to make ourselves better. And whatever money is left after I'm gone will be yours someday. I want you to use it and to build a better life than I did, and your children should have a better life than you have. That's the way things should be."

"You don't have to do that," we told her again.

"I'm doing it," Oma said. "So shut the bleep up."

Oma was pretty upset when Dad told her he had torn up Silverman's contract. But when we told her all the things Silverman was going to do to make money off her, even she agreed that it wasn't a good idea to be involved.

"Over my bleeping dead body will he put me in a diaper ad," she said.

As it turned out, Oma didn't need Silverman anyway. After her appearance on the TV news, the phone just kept ringing. Offers started pouring in from all over. Silverman wasn't the only one out there who saw the moneymaking possibilities of "Slap-Shot Sophie."

First it was the hockey companies. Somebody

wanted to put Oma's picture on a puck. They wanted her to give exhibitions at games and sign autographs at stores. They wanted to market a line of hockey jerseys for senior citizens.

Then we started getting calls from "the old fogey companies," as Oma called them. They wanted her to endorse electric wheelchairs, walkers, and beds that have motors in them to help you get up. They wanted to put her on the cover of *Modern Maturity* magazine.

The coolest thing was that after articles about Oma appeared in the local papers, the kids at school started treating me like I was a celebrity. They would ask for autographs and tickets to see the Canadiens. Kids would come up to me in the hallway and say, "Hey, aren't you the kid whose grandmother is going to take that million dollar shot?" And when I said I was, they would say something like, "Dude, your grandma rocks!"

Kids at school started saying *bleep* all the time because they'd seen Oma get bleeped out on TV. They didn't even say the real curse words that had been bleeped. They'd just say "bleep" instead, as a sort of meaningless word that could be used in any situation.

"Hey, bleep! You want to bleeping go for a bleeping piece of pizza after bleeping school? I'll bleeping meet you at my bleeping locker when the bleeping bell rings." It was hilarious.

Dad had to take some days off from work because he needed to spend so much time fielding requests for Oma to go on talk shows, meet with publishers, respond to e-mail, and decide which offers to accept and which ones to turn down. He was even getting calls from the American media, which hardly ever covers news in Canada.

Every day, Oma was getting more famous. People just seemed to think it was intriguing or amusing or something that this eighty-year-old lady in a wheelchair would be trying to shoot a hockey puck into a goal for a million dollars.

"Oma is one of those irresistible human-interest stories they fill space with when there's no big news to report," Dad told us. "If a war broke out tomorrow, nobody would be writing about her."

One night, we were just sitting down to eat dinner when the phone rang. Usually when people call at dinnertime, they're trying to sell you something and we don't pick up the phone. But there had been so many calls about Oma lately that Dad felt we should take the call. He asked me to pick it up.

"Is this the Rosenberg residence?" a lady asked.

"We're not interested," I said wearily and hung up the phone. The lady had the unmistakable sound of a telemarketer.

A few seconds later, the phone rang again. I picked it up. It was the same lady. I was about to tell her to leave us alone, but she said, "Wait! Could you pass the telephone over to Mrs. Sophie Rosenberg, please?"

I gave Oma the phone and went to the dinner table. She listened for a minute or two and then mumbled something and joined us at the table.

"Who was that, Oma?" Mom asked. "One of your fans?"

"Yeah, the Queen," she said as she filled her plate.

We all stopped eating.

"What Queen?" Dad asked.

"How many bleeping Queens are there?" Oma said. "It was the Queen of England. She said she heard about me and told me good luck and all that nonsense."

After that, it was impossible to eat. I realized that I was probably the only person in the world who ever had hung up on the Queen of England!

ALL SHOOK UP

With each practice session, Oma was getting better and better. And with each practice session, more and more people were gathering on the sidewalk outside our house to watch her shoot puck after puck into the net.

"She bleeping shoots!" the crowd would holler. "She bleeping scores!"

Watching Oma practice had become a community event, like fireworks or a parade. People brought their own folding lawn chairs, and they'd come early to make sure they got a good seat. Busloads of senior citizens from nearby retirement communities would pull up to the curb and they would all pile out to cheer Oma on. Schools were even sending kids on class trips to our house. One day I counted fifty spectators out there. We could have set up bleachers and charged admission.

While she was practicing, the spectators would all be staring and pointing and taking pictures of Oma. She must have felt like she was an animal in a zoo. One guy would come every day and hold up a sign that said BLEEPING BLEEP BLEEP BLEEP!

Dad sold all the T-shirts he had printed and he had to reorder. We set up a little booth where people could buy the shirts, and we kept running out.

When people came by and Oma wasn't outside practicing, they would start to chant, "Oma! Oma! Oma!" until she would roll over to the window and give them a little wave.

Word got around that Oma idolized Elvis Presley, and soon people were giving her Elvis key chains, Elvis pot holders, and all kinds of silly Elvis memorabilia. Night and day, Elvis impersonators would stand on the sidewalk with guitars and serenade Oma with bad renditions of Elvis songs. Our neighbors called the cops a few times because they couldn't sleep.

A bunch of people asked Oma if she would sell them that awful Velvet Elvis that was hanging over our living-room couch. It had become one of those things that was so uncool, it was cool.

"It's not for sale," Oma told them. "The King gave me that himself, and he said it would bring me good luck."

Some magazine named Oma their "Grandmother of the Year." She was getting marriage proposals from lonely widowers. In a few short weeks, she had become the most famous woman in Canada.

Oma pretended none of this affected her. She would shout to the people hanging around outside our house, "Go home, you bleeping losers!" and "Get a bleeping life!" And they loved her for it!

But you could tell that deep down inside, she liked all the attention and encouragement. It seemed to give her more energy, more determination. I had never seen her so full of life. Her eyes were brighter. I was really starting to believe that she might actually make the shot and win that million dollars.

It was only a week and a half before the big night and everything was looking good. We had just had a practice in which Oma was nailing shot after shot, each one stronger than the one before it.

Then, just as she was about to unload a shot, I heard a crack. Oma's wheelchair toppled over and she fell out of it onto the driveway, landing on her right side, her shooting side. I thought the crack I heard must have been a bone breaking.

Rocket and I and about a dozen people who were watching rushed to Oma's side. A man used his cell phone to call for an ambulance. Some of the people on the street began sobbing.

Just like the first time she had fallen down, the paramedics picked Oma up carefully, put her on a stretcher, and rushed her to the hospital.

When I told a paramedic what had happened, he turned the wheelchair upside down to see what had gone wrong. I figured the wheel must have become loosened or something like that. Maybe the whole thing was our fault. Rocket and I should have been more careful to see that Oma's wheelchair was in good condition.

"This wheel isn't loose," the paramedic told me. "That crack you heard was the axle breaking. Somebody sawed almost right through the thing."

SUSPICIOUS MINDS

Rocket and I rode to the hospital in the ambulance (which was pretty cool, even though they refused to turn on the siren). Oma was not in pain the way she had been the last time she fell down. In fact, she didn't want to go to the hospital at all. She insisted that she was fine, and she kept yelling at the driver to turn around and take her home. But the paramedics said that just to be on the safe side, a doctor should examine Oma.

"Don't ever grow old," she advised me, taking my hand with her papery fingers. "Because every time you fall down, they take you to the bleeping hospital."

One of the paramedics let me use her cell phone so I could call Mom and Dad at work. They arrived at the hospital just a few minutes after we did. Oma was taken to her room and in a few minutes the doctor came in. It was Dr. Patel, the same guy who examined Oma the last time she fell down.

"Mrs. Rosenberg, so nice to see you again!" Dr. Patel said. "I have been reading in the newspapers that you've been playing a lot of hockey. Are you going to be trying out for the Canadiens?"

"I'm perfectly all right," Oma complained. "Let me out of here."

"Not before you give me your autograph," Dr. Patel said as he began to push against Oma's arms and legs to see if she felt any pain.

The doctor asked us to leave the room for a few minutes so they could have some privacy. We really didn't want to see Oma naked anyway, to be honest. Rocket and I went out in the hall with Mom and Dad to tell them what had happened.

"The chair just collapsed?" Dad asked, puzzled. "The wheels must have been loose."

"They weren't loose, Dad," Rocket told him. "Somebody took a hacksaw and cut a groove halfway through the axle. I saw it. It was just a matter of time until it snapped."

It was hard for us to grasp the idea that anyone would intentionally hurt an old lady.

"Maybe we should call the police," I suggested.

"No," Dad said, rubbing his chin. "I think we can figure this out on our own."

This is when Dad went into his Sherlock Holmes routine. He has read just about every detective novel ever written, so he thinks he can solve any crime.

Dad started pacing up and down the corridor, speculating on the motive, weapons, and what suspect could have possibly committed this heinous crime. It was hysterical. And to think he was wasting his life coming up with dumb slogans for pizza places.

First Dad guessed that the criminal might be the management of the Montreal Canadiens, because they had a perfect motive—if Oma missed the shot, they wouldn't have to pay her a million dollars. So they figured that if Oma was injured, she would miss the shot. They must have sawed through the axle, or hired someone else to do it for them.

We all agreed that was a ridiculous theory. Although some of the players on the team had been accused of being thugs on the ice, the

Canadiens were a reputable organization and wouldn't lower themselves to such dirty tricks.

Dad's next theory was that it might be a hate crime. It had been all over the papers that Oma was Jewish, and maybe some anti-Semite had decided to sabotage her chances of making the million dollar goal.

Again, a very unlikely possibility. If some bigots wanted to get Oma, they would do something a lot worse than making her fall out of her wheelchair. And they didn't burn a cross on our front lawn or paint swastikas on the garage door or anything like that. There was no evidence of a hate crime.

Personally, I thought it was some Elvis Presley haters who did it. Ever since Oma had become famous, they'd been playing that awful Elvis music on the radio constantly. Maybe hearing "Heartbreak Hotel" for the thousandth time had driven somebody off the deep end and they couldn't take it anymore, so they had decided to take it out on Oma.

Are you finished?

No.

"I've got it!" Dad finally said, snapping his fingers.

We had to sit in suspense for a few minutes, because Dr. Patel came out of Oma's room.

"I have good news and bad news," he told us. "The good news is that your Oma is okay. She's an indestructible woman, in fact. She's like one of those piñatas that refuses to break no matter how many times you hit it."

I knew that was true.

"What's the bad news, doctor?" Mom asked, all worried.

"The bad news is that she refused to give me her autograph," Dr. Patel replied. "And while I was examining her, she farted on me."

We all laughed except for Rocket, who rolled his eyes and pretended to stick his finger down his throat and throw up.

Dad's brilliant plan was to set a trap to catch the "wheelchair saboteur" red-handed. It would be a "sting operation," as he called it. That night, after we had brought Oma home and put her to bed, Dad led us out to the driveway. The broken wheelchair was still out there, sitting on the plastic ice.

Dad had four folding chairs with him, and he set them up around the wheelchair. Then he pulled some of that bright yellow crime-scene tape out of his pocket, the kind of tape the police put up to keep people away from touching things. It said WARNING all over the tape.

"This is the bait," he told us excitedly, as he wrapped the tape around the circle of chairs. "Criminals always return to the scene of their crimes. The person or people who vandalized Oma's wheelchair will come back. When they see the wheelchair sitting out here unprotected, it will be irresistible to them. I'm betting they will try to wipe off their fingerprints or maybe even steal the whole wheelchair. And when they do, we've got them!"

"So you're going to sit out here hiding all night and watching for somebody to show up?" Mom asked.

"No, that's the beauty of my plan," Dad said. "I don't have to sit out here all night."

Dad took his little video camera out of his coat pocket.

"*This* is going to sit out here all night and do the watching *for* me!"

We all thought it was a pretty dumb plan. First of all, whoever had sawed through Oma's axle wasn't likely to show up again. Criminals only return to the scene of the crime in movies and detective novels. In the real world, they just go find somebody else to victimize. Secondly, the battery of the video camera wouldn't last all night. And finally, well, it was just plain silly. Whoever had vandalized the wheelchair wouldn't know it was still out there in the driveway, waiting to be revisited.

But Dad was all excited that he was finally getting the chance to put his amateur detective skills to work. He sent me back to the house to get his tripod and put the video camera on the tripod. Then he hid it behind a bush. He put in a blank cassette, turned the camera on, and we all went back home to go to sleep.

First thing in the morning, Dad went out to see if the wheelchair or the crime-scene tape had been tampered with. They hadn't. When he came back in the house with his video camera and tripod, he almost seemed like he was disappointed that nobody had stolen the wheelchair so he would have been able to catch them on video.

We were all making fun of Dad and telling him how sorry we were that his brilliant detective work hadn't solved the crime of the century. Dad said he would rewind the cassette and try again that night.

Rocket wanted to watch the tape, but Dad said it was pointless. If the wheelchair hadn't been moved, there would be nothing of interest on it.

I just thought it would be a riot to watch a video of all that stuff sitting in the driveway all night.

It was. Rocket plunked the cassette in the VCR, and of course it was exactly what we expected it to be. There was a wheelchair surrounded by four other chairs sitting in the driveway. The moon lit the scene just enough to see it. The chairs didn't move. Nothing happened. I've seen some pretty boring videos on MTV, but this had to be the most boring one in the history of the world.

Rocket fast-forwarded to the middle, and it was more of the same. I suggested the title of the movie be *A Night in the Life of Five Chairs*. Mom said that Dad should get an Oscar for best director. Rocket said the video had more action than the last three *Star Wars* movies. It was hilarious.

"You've got to see this!" Rocket cracked when absolutely nothing was happening. "This is my favorite part!"

Dad was pretty good-natured about the kidding. But soon we all got tired of making fun of him, and he went to turn the VCR off. Just before he pushed the STOP button, we heard something on the video.

A sound. It was the sound of a car engine.

The engine turned off and we heard the sound of a car door shutting. Then the sound of footsteps.

"Who could that be in the middle of the night?" Mom wondered.

The footsteps got louder, and then you could hear them slipping on the plastic ice. Somebody was creeping around outside our house.

"Uh-huh!" Dad said excitedly. "You all laugh at me, but I told you the criminal returns to the scene of the crime!"

We kept watching, and suddenly a figure appeared in the frame. It looked to be a man. He was wearing a hat. He was facing the other way so we couldn't see his face. He was examining the crime-scene tape.

"Turn around!" we all yelled at the screen.

The guy tried to step over the tape, but as he lifted one leg the other one slipped and he fell down. The tape didn't break when he hit it, but it pulled the chairs a little bit closer together. Quickly, the guy got up and fixed the chairs. The fall must have spooked him, because he ran away. As he was running, he turned around to face the camera for a split second. We couldn't make out his face. He ran back to his car and drove away.

"Rewind that!" Dad instructed Rocket.

Rocket backed the video up to the point where the guy fell down, and then played it forward in slow motion.

"Pause it right . . . *there!*" Dad barked the moment the guy turned around to face the camera.

There was a cigar in his mouth. It was Sheldon Silverman.

13

LOVE ME TENDER

I wasn't there. I wish I had been there so I could have seen it. But Sheldon Silverman was arrested. They even found in his car the hacksaw that he'd used to cut through Oma's axle.

It said in the newspaper that Silverman made quite a scene, ranting and raving about how he was the one who had made Oma famous, and our family had stolen his money. They showed him on the news being led away in handcuffs. It was great.

"I told you that guy was a sleazeball," Dad said. "I hope they put him away for a good long time."

Dad had to go to the police station to give them evidence against Silverman, and he loved every second of it. I think it made him feel like a real crime buster. He was in a great mood.

Oma wasn't feeling so well that morning, so we didn't take her with us on an important errand. We had to go to the Molson Centre to iron out the details of the million dollar goal. All that the Canadiens had told us so far was that Oma would be taking a shot for a million dollars. We didn't know exactly how far she would be shooting from, or any other specifics about the evening.

Mom wanted me or Rocket to stay home with Oma, but we begged her to take us along. We both wanted to walk on the same ice the Canadiens skate on.

I wanted to bring along my skates in case I would be allowed to take a few laps around the rink, but Dad said no way.

We were met at the Molson Centre by a lady named Debbie Dunn, the public-relations director of the Canadiens. She had a big cheery smile on her face and made some lame joke about "breaking the ice." She said she was disappointed that the famous Sophie "Bleep Bleep" Rosenberg had not been able to make it, but she was happy to show us exactly what was going to happen on Saturday night so we could tell Oma.

I had been inside the Molson Centre plenty of

times before to see hockey games, but this was different. Every seat in the place was empty now. It felt colder. Whenever you said anything, your voice echoed off the walls. It was kind of creepy.

Miss Dunn led us out onto the ice, the same ice all my hockey heroes from the past had skated on. Wayne Gretzky had probably stood right here on this ice, I marveled. So had Bobby Hull, Gordie Howe, and all the others.

Ice is ice. I'm sure it all melted away and has been resurfaced a thousand times since those guys played here.

Rocket is such a bore. Anyway, we went out to center ice. Miss Dunn cautioned us to be careful not to slip and fall. She told us that the February twenty-first game was already a sellout. If Oma made the million dollar goal, they were going to make a big deal with lights, lasers, fireworks, and all that stuff.

"How far will my mother have to shoot from?" Dad asked.

"Right here," Miss Dunn said. "The red line. It's the exact center point of the stadium. We want to make sure all the fans get a great view. We'll set up the target fifty feet from this spot."

Dad looked over at me and Rocket to see our reactions.

"She can do it," I assured him, measuring off the distance in my head and comparing it to our driveway.

"Piece of cake," Rocket added.

"Wonderful!" Miss Dunn said. "Now, I want to make sure you folks understand that Mrs. Rosenberg will not be shooting at a regular goal."

"What will she be shooting at?" Mom asked.

"A check," Miss Dunn replied. "For a million dollars. It will be made out in her name. If she hits the check, she gets to keep it. We thought that would be much more exciting than having her just shooting at a meaningless target."

"Wait a minute!" Dad said, holding up his hand like a traffic cop. "How big will this check be?"

"You know, a regular-size check," she replied, holding her two index fingers about six inches apart.

I looked across the ice again. Fifty feet. A six-inch target. Rocket or I might be able to make that shot one time out of ten with a little luck. Oma had no chance.

"You must be joking!" Dad said, veins popping out on his neck. "That's a virtually impossible shot! My mother has been in the hospital twice because of this contest. She has been out there every day for a month practicing."

"Then she has an excellent chance," Miss Dunn said, still smiling, but not quite as sweetly as when she had said hello to us.

Dad looked like he was just about ready to explode, but Mom held him back and calmed him down.

"You mentioned your concern about the fans being able to see," she said to Miss Dunn politely. "But how are they going to be able to see a tiny little check?"

"We'll make it neon yellow," Miss Dunn replied, "and we'll show it up on the JumboTron screen."

"Wouldn't it be a better idea to have her shoot at one of those giant checks?" Mom suggested, holding her hands out as far apart as she could. "I see that on TV all the time, when companies donate money to charities."

"This is not a charity," Miss Dunn said, no longer smiling. "It's a contest."

"Miss Dunn," Mom said, changing her strategy,

"my children are loyal fans of the Canadiens. . . ."

Miss Dunn just shrugged.

Dad couldn't restrain himself any longer. "This is a big scam, isn't it?" he said, getting in Miss Dunn's face. "You can't expect an old lady in a wheelchair to make a shot like that! What kind of a flimflam operation are you people running here? I'm going to call my lawyer!"

"I would like to help you, Mr. Rosenberg." Miss Dunn was all serious-looking now. "But we're talking about giving away a million dollars here. That's a lot of money. You can't expect us to make the shot *easy*. If your mother doesn't want to participate in the contest with the rules as we have set them up, she doesn't have to."

I was hoping that Dad would take that lady's contract, rip it up, and throw it in her face, just like he did with that creep Silverman's contract. That would have been cool.

I guess he decided that one chance in a million was better than no chance at all. He signed the paperwork, being careful to read all the small print to make sure they weren't trying to pull any other underhanded schemes on us.

We were all bummed out in the car on the way

home. Up until this point, we all thought Oma had a decent chance of scoring the goal. Now we knew she had virtually no chance. There was no way she was going to be able to hit a target so small. None of us wanted to break the news to her.

As it turned out, we didn't have to. Approaching our street, we heard a siren wailing and then we saw an ambulance parked in front of our house. A bunch of gawkers were gathered on the sidewalk.

Dad screeched the car to a stop and we all ran out. A paramedic came out the front door just as Mom was about to open it.

"I'm sorry," he said, tears rolling down his cheeks. "Mrs. Rosenberg is dead."

14

JAILHOUSE ROCK

We all cried, of course. Even Rocket. Dad just sank to his knees right in the doorway when we got the news that Oma had died.

I knew all along that she didn't have many years ahead of her. We never spoke about it, of course. But every New Year's Eve I used to wonder whether or not Oma would still be with us for the next New Year's Eve. I guess she wasn't indestructible after all. Nobody is.

"Turn off the siren, guys," the paramedic told the ambulance driver. Once they know somebody is dead, I guess there's no reason to rush to the hospital.

I had never seen a dead person before. But I caught a glimpse of Oma. She was lying in her bed.

She looked so peaceful there, like she was sleeping. But I didn't want to touch her. I couldn't bear the thought that her hand might be cold.

I didn't look. I didn't want to.

The paramedics told us that Oma had called the hospital about half an hour earlier, complaining that she was having trouble breathing. They had gotten there a few minutes later and done all they could to save her, but it was no use. They guessed it was a heart attack, but a doctor would have to make that decision.

"Did she have any last words?" Mom asked one of the paramedics who had tried to revive Oma.

"Yes," he said. "She asked me to lean over close to her, and then she whispered in my ear, 'Elvis lives.'" The paramedic broke down, sobbing.

By the time they carried Oma out of the house, our street was filled with people. The word had already spread. People were arriving with flowers, newspaper clippings about Oma, hockey memorabilia, and all kinds of things. They arranged them neatly on our lawn, turning it into a memorial to Oma. People were crying and playing Elvis Presley songs on their boom boxes.

I never realized that when people die, there are a lot of things that their loved ones have to do. Even though the family is incredibly sad, they have to quickly arrange for a funeral, meet with a lawyer to go over the will, track down keys and bankbooks, and other things. We had to arrange to have Oma's name carved on the headstone she would share with Poppop.

Mom had to do most of this stuff, because Dad was pretty broken up. He and Oma used to fight all the time, but I could see he really loved her too. I guess Mom was right when she said that sometimes you love somebody even if you didn't particularly like them.

Rocket and I were pretty broken up too. In the short time we had been working with Oma to get her ready for her million dollar goal, we had gotten to know her well for the first time. While she could be tough to get along with sometimes, we found that she was really an incredible woman. She was tough, she was determined, she really cared about us, and sometimes she was even funny.

I felt really bad because before the whole million dollar goal thing, I had been wishing Oma would die so we wouldn't have to deal with her anymore. And now she was dead and, well, I just felt terrible.

The story about Oma was already flashing around the Internet and the TV news that afternoon. The prime minister declared it a national day of mourning. People from all over Canada started calling to offer their condolences. We had to take the phone off the hook or it would have been ringing constantly.

Mom didn't feel like cooking that night, so we went out to a little pizza place not far from our house. We were all pretty depressed and nobody had much to say. I was in the middle of my second slice of pizza when the thought crossed my mind—what about the million dollar goal?

I felt a little ashamed about having that thought. Oma hadn't even been buried yet, and there I was already wondering in the back of my mind if maybe I might be able to take the shot in her place.

You didn't have to feel ashamed. I had the same thought, and I was only on my first slice of pizza. But there was no way I was going to bring it up. I thought Dad would flip.

As it turned out, neither of us had to bring it up, because Mom did.

"Do you think they'll call the contest off?" she asked.

"I wonder," Dad said. He reached into his jacket pocket and pulled out the paperwork he had signed when we were at the Molson Centre earlier in the day. He had to look it over very carefully before he found this passage, which Dad read out loud: "'. . . and in the event of the death of the participant prior to the contest, a member of the immediate family may, if he or she wishes, take the place of the original partici-pant. . . .'"

Dad looked at me and Rocket. I looked at Rocket. Rocket looked at me.

Then we all looked at the door to the pizza place, because three policemen came in. They didn't look like they wanted pizza. They looked all serious. And they came right over to our table. I figured they were coming over to offer their con-dolences.

"Mr. Rosenberg," one cop said, putting a hand on Dad's shoulder, "I'm sorry to tell you this, but we need to bring you in for questioning."

"Questioning?" Dad asked, startled. "This must be some mistake. I've never broken the law in my life! What's the charge?"

"You are wanted for questioning concerning the death of Sophie Rosenberg."

MY WISH CAME TRUE

Dad jumped out of his seat and began yelling at the policemen. One of them put an arm around him roughly to hold him back. Mom was screaming at them to let Dad go. He bumped the table with his leg and his plate fell off and shattered against the floor.

Everybody in the restaurant turned around to watch. I had never been so embarrassed in my life. Two of the policemen were holding Dad now. I had never seen him so angry. I was afraid things might get out of hand and the cops might hit him over the head with their nightsticks or something. If it had been any other dad in the world, I would have thought it was cool. I mean, this was better than any hockey fight I had ever seen. But it was my dad, and I was scared.

Dad was almost out of control. And who could blame him? That morning his mother had died, and now he was being brought in for questioning as if he had killed her, or something. I nearly went berserk myself, but Mom told me and Rocket to sit down and keep quiet.

Dad finally calmed down and was led out to the police car. Mom brought us home and told us to go to sleep, but I couldn't sleep, of course. All I could think about was my father in jail, maybe for the rest of his life.

In the end, Dad didn't go to jail at all. He was questioned at the police station and he was home before midnight. The policemen who brought him home apologized over and over again for the "inconvenience" they had caused.

"It was because of Silverman," Dad explained after the cops had left. "When he heard the news that Oma had died, he e-mailed in an anonymous tip that I poisoned her so that one of you kids would get to shoot the million dollar goal in her place and we'd have a better chance of winning the money. He must have wanted to get revenge on me for sending him to jail. Can you believe that? That guy must be insane."

"How did they know it was Silverman who sent in the e-mail?" Mom asked.

"They traced it to his jail. And when they got the results back from the tests and found there was no poison in Oma's body, they knew Silverman was lying. I'm surprised he didn't think to have her poisoned too. If he had done that, I would be in jail right now."

It was late. It had been a long, hard day. The next day would be the funeral. We had a family hug and Mom made Dad a cup of tea to calm his nerves.

I didn't want to go to bed just yet. The four of us sat on the living-room couch under Velvet Elvis. I wondered if it would be wrong to get rid of it now that Oma was gone.

"I know we're all thinking about Oma right now," Dad said before sending us up to bed, "but there's something we need to talk about. There are five days left until the million dollar goal. Your mother and I don't know the first thing about hockey. Which one of you wants to take the shot?"

"I do!" we both said at the exact same time.

"I'm a better shooter," Rocket claimed.

"No, you aren't."

"Yes, I am."

"I'm older."

"Yeah, by three minutes!"

"You can't both take the shot," Mom said. "One of you is going to have to be disappointed. You have to come up with a fair solution you can both live with."

"Rock paper scissors?" Rocket suggested.

"You always cheat," I said.

"Draw straws?"

"We could flip a coin," I suggested.

"Fine," Rocket said. "Whatever."

"I have another idea," Mom said. "Why don't you have some kind of a . . . shootout?"

A shootout. Yeah. Rocket and I were nodding our heads. Flipping a coin would be fair too, of course. We'd each have a fifty-fifty chance of winning a coin toss. But for the million dollar goal, it should be the best shooter in there. Plain and simple. And the only way to find out which one of us was the best shooter would be to have a shootout.

"Let me say this," Dad said, "Just so there are no

hard feelings, I think that whichever one of you wins the shootout should split the million dollars evenly with the other one. That is, of course, assuming you score the goal. Can you both agree to that?"

"Agreed," we said, and we shook on it.

The next day we went to Oma's funeral, which was held at a synagogue nearby. Thousands of people, many of them we didn't even know, came to pay their respects. It was all very sad, of course. When the Elvis impersonator came out to talk about Oma and sing "Love Me Tender," everybody was in tears. We were still getting over it late into the night. Rocket and I felt a little bit guilty having our shootout the day after Oma's funeral, but we both agreed that Oma would have wanted us to get on with our lives.

First thing in the morning, Mom called up our hockey coaches. Rocket's coach was on vacation. But Mom reached Phil Cutrone, my coach. Coach Cutrone had been to the funeral, and was wondering what was going to happen with the million dollar goal. Mom told him about the shootout between me and Rocket, and he agreed to help. He told Mom to bring us over to St-Michel, the rink where our team practices, that night after dinner.

I figured it would be me and Rocket, our parents, and Coach Cutrone. But when we pulled into the St-Michel parking lot, it was hard to find a spot. The place was jammed with people. And when we walked into the rink, a roar went up from the bleachers. I looked around and saw all the girls on my team, all the guys on Rocket's team, lots of kids from school, just about everybody we knew, and a whole bunch of strangers too. Some people were holding up pictures of Oma.

Coach Cutrone must have spread the word by phone or e-mail or something. There must have been a thousand people there! It was scary.

It was cool! Usually a dozen spectators or so show up at our games—our parents. I felt my blood pumping when we stepped out on the ice in front of all those people. All the guys on my team were sitting on one side of the rink, and all the girls on Dawn's team were sitting on the other side.

"Go get him, Dawn!" My teammates were hollering and hooting and whistling.

"Dusk, you're the man!" countered his teammates.

Before we went out on the ice, Mom and Dad

pulled us aside for a minute to give us the old whichever-one-of-you-wins-we-still-love-you-both-blah-blah-blah talk. They are so cliché.

Coach Cutrone led us out to center ice. There were two pucks out there on the red line. At the other end of the rink were two shoe boxes, each with one side cut away. It was obvious that Rocket and I would each be trying to shoot a puck into a shoe box.

Coach Cutrone had already talked things over with our parents and worked out the details. Rocket and I would take turns, each shooting ten shots at a distance of fifty feet. He was trying to duplicate the conditions one of us would face on Saturday night in the Molson Centre.

After ten shots, whichever one of us had gotten the puck in the shoe box the most times would be the winner. If it was a tie, or if neither of us got it in the shoe box in ten shots, we would have a sudden-death overtime. The first one to get one in the shoe box would be the winner.

"The puck must go in the shoe box to count as a goal," Coach Cutrone explained. "Are you kids ready?"

"Don't we get a warm-up?" I asked.

"They won't be giving you a warm-up on Saturday night," Coach Cutrone reminded me. "Whichever one of you can handle this kind of pressure should get the chance to shoot the million dollar goal."

The Coach flipped a coin to see who would shoot first, and Rocket won. That was okay with me. I didn't want to shoot first. Let Rocket take that pressure.

I wanted to go first. When I stepped up to the puck for my first shot, everybody was screaming their heads off. I took a deep bow to both sides of the bleachers and waved like I was a big celebrity. I was eating it up!

Yeah, and then he missed his first shot by about twenty feet! Normally I would have laughed. But I figured I should be cool about it because I might do the very same thing. I didn't, though. I missed to the right by about three feet.

Rocket stepped up for his next shot, and this time he didn't clown for the crowd. He was all business. His shot was right there. I thought it was a score, but it missed the shoe box by a couple of inches on the right. The crowd let out a big "Ooooooh!" and Rocket pounded the ice with his stick.

I lined up for my next shot. My first one had been off to the right, so I figured I had to make a correction. I aimed a little bit to the left. That's where it went. A little bit to the left.

This is a tough shot, I was thinking. How would one of us score on Saturday night with just one chance if we couldn't do it in ten chances tonight?

I was thinking these thoughts when Rocket's third shot slid into the shoe box.

"Goooooooooooooooaaaaaaaaaaaaalllll!" screamed about five hundred people. Rocket pumped his fist the way Tiger Woods does when he sinks a big putt. People were shouting congratulations to Rocket and encouragement to me.

"Boys rule! Girls drool!" the guys on Rocket's hockey team chanted.

It was my turn. I tried to pull myself together. Negative thoughts produce negative results. That's what Coach Cutrone always told us. I'm as good a shot as Rocket. If he can score, I can score.

My shot just missed, a few inches to the right. He had me 1–0 after three shots. There was still plenty of time to catch up.

Both of us missed our next two shots, but just by a few inches. We were in the zone. I was getting more comfortable. The crowd was still shouting, but they weren't as distracting to me as they had been at first. I was focusing on the target. When Rocket missed his sixth shot and mine slid right into the middle of the shoe box, I let out a scream.

"Goooooooooooooooaaaaaaaaaaaaaallll!"

"Girls go to college to get more knowledge!" my teammates chanted. "Boys go to Jupiter to get more stupider!"

The score was 1–1 with four shots left. Rocket skated over to me, a determined look on his face.

"You're gonna lose," he said, or some other macho thing he'd undoubtedly heard in one of those action-hero movies he watches. He was trying to intimidate me. I just laughed. I had lived with my brother for eleven years. He wasn't about to intimidate me. I had seen him dancing in his underpants to a Barney tape.

What I said was, "You're going down." And you were so nervous you were shaking in your skates.

Whatever. Rocket slipped his next shot into the shoe box and the pressure was on me, especially after I missed my shot. We both missed our eighth and ninth shots.

One shot left. It didn't take a math genius to

know that with a 2–1 lead, if Rocket scored on his last shot, he would win.

His teammates were shouting out advice and Rocket lined up the shot. I put my hands over my eyes because I couldn't bear to watch. When I heard the "Ooooooh!" from the crowd, I knew he'd missed.

It was 2–1 and I had one last chance to tie it up. I took a deep breath to calm myself. The crowd was screaming, clapping, stomping their feet against the wooden bleachers. I had never been under so much pressure in my life.

"You can do it, Dawn!" somebody screamed.

I lined up the puck and smacked it. And guess what?

It went in.

"Goooooooooooooooaaaaaaaaaaaaaallll!"

The whole place was going crazy and I was going crazy and Mom and Dad were going crazy too. People were throwing teddy bears and stuff onto the ice.

This must be what it feels like to win the Stanley Cup, I thought. The Super Bowl. The World Series. The Olympics. The Tour de France. Wimbledon. The Masters.

"Okay," Coach Cutrone said, throwing an arm around each of us. "You both scored two goals in ten shots. That was good. Now it's sudden death. The next one to score a goal is the winner. Dusk, you won the coin toss, so you're up."

I would like to say we had a long, tension-filled sudden-death playoff. I would like to say that. But I can't. Rocket's first overtime shot hit the target, and he won the shootout.

Dawn was a little bit upset that she didn't win, and I couldn't blame her. I had eleven shots, and she only had ten. If she'd had the chance to take another shot, there was a good possibility that she would have scored. But it was sudden death, and that's the way it goes.

It had been a good battle. After it was over, everybody was hugging everybody else. Dawn told me I'd won it fair and square, and she would support me all the way. She was really happy for me.

Me, I had no time to celebrate. I only had a few days to get ready for the million dollar goal.

16

IF I CAN DREAM

I don't think it was until the day after the shoot-out that reality finally sank in—Rocket would get the chance to shoot a puck at a target, and if he hit the target the two of us would split a million dollars. Suddenly, the million dollar goal was real.

A million dollars! This wasn't a CD or ice cream or some cheap stuffed animal prize you win at a carnival. It was a million dollars! That's more money than I can imagine. You can buy a lot of stuff for a million dollars. Just about anything you want.

Rocket and I had a long talk about what we would do with the money if we won it. He was thinking along the lines of cool cars and giant screen TVs and all-terrain vehicles and stuff like that. I told him that was silly. He's not even old enough to drive a car if he had one.

I was thinking of putting the money away for college or maybe starting a charity for elderly women like Oma. Rocket said I was out of my mind. He said we should enjoy the money. Oma would have wanted us to, he insisted.

In the end, we decided that we should use the money to build a regulation-size hockey rink in the field behind our house. All the kids we knew could come over and play hockey whenever they liked. We would call it the Sophie Rosenberg Memorial Rink. That seemed like a good idea.

"Two expressions come to mind," Dad said when we told him about our plans. "The first one is 'Cross that bridge when you get to it.' The second one is, 'Don't count your chickens before they're hatched.'"

Dad is so cliché. But he was right, of course. We were too confident. At the shootout, Rocket had only made three goals out of eleven shots. We used a calculator to figure out his shooting percentage: .27272727. A little better than one out of four. Not all that good.

Mom dropped us off at St-Michel ice rink after school on Wednesday so Rocket could practice. The owner had told her that we could come over anytime we wanted, even during figure skating lessons. I guess he thought it would be good publicity for St-Michel if Rocket was seen there.

There were a few figure skaters practicing their spins and jumps. They were watching and whispering, but nobody bothered us. We had a good practice. I acted as Rocket's helper, feeding him puck after puck. He aimed for a spot in the boards fifty feet away.

When he was able to hit that about half the time, I bought him a can of soda as a reward. He drained it, and then I put it on the ice to see if he could knock it over from fifty feet. A couple of times, he did.

While we were practicing, the thought crossed my mind that if Oma hadn't died, I wouldn't be doing this. I would be helping Oma prepare for her million dollar goal. And it would be her money to win.

I was thinking the exact same thing. It's a twin thing, I guess.

When he got tired, Rocket skated over to me.

"Do you remember Oma's last words?" he asked.

"Elvis lives," I recalled. "So what?"

"Elvis lives. It's like an anagram or something. If you scramble the letters in 'Elvis,' it spells 'lives.' Same letters in both words. See?"

"You're not going to get creepy on me now, are you?" I asked.

I was just wondering why Oma would have said that. It had to mean something. Like, maybe she saw Elvis on the other side as she was dying.

Fortunately, Dad showed up to take us home before Rocket could creep me out any further. Dad was holding a long, thin cardboard box about as tall as we are, and he handed it to Rocket. He tore it open. Inside were two hockey sticks.

"One for each of you," Dad said. "The guy in the store said they are made of some state-of-the-art composite material."

"These are top-of-the-line sticks like the pros use!" Rocket marveled, examining his carefully. "Thanks, Dad!"

"You mean to say that you actually set foot into a hockey store?" I asked, incredulous. "All our lives you've been telling us how you can't stand hockey! You refused to learn the game. You made us buy our own equipment. Why the sudden change?"

"Maybe you can teach an old dog new tricks," Dad said, taking my new stick in his hand. "I've learned a thing or two this past month. You know, the guy in the store told me that if you hold your right hand closer to the blade like this, it should improve your accuracy."

"Now you're going to tell *me* how to shoot?" Rocket asked. We all had a good laugh over that, and Dad walked us out to the parking lot with one arm around each of us.

IT'S NOW OR NEVER

Saturday morning. February twenty-first. This was it. The big day. No turning back. Now or never. And all those other clichés.

Rocket didn't have much to eat for breakfast, I noticed. He didn't feel like watching cartoons on TV. He was just wandering around the house with nothing to do. I asked him if he wanted to take a few practice shots out on the pond, but he didn't want to do that, either.

Hey, I figured that if I didn't have my shot by then, I probably never would have it. I just wanted to shoot the thing.

Fortunately, we were told to get to the Molson Centre early, so we didn't have to hang around the house all day. I was probably as nervous as Rocket when we were getting ready to leave. I'm not sure if he was throwing up, but he was in the bathroom for an awfully long time.

I did not throw up and I was not nervous. I was combing my hair. When you've got twenty thousand people watching you, you want to look good out there.

"Are you going to wear your Canadiens jersey or the one with your name on it?" Mom asked while we were waiting for Rocket to get out of the bathroom.

"Neither," Rocket said. Then he came out wearing one of the yellow T-shirts Dad had made with Oma's picture on it.

Before we left the house, Dad gave Rocket the old whether-you-make-the-shot-or-miss-it-we'll-still-love-you-blah-blah-blah talk. He is so cliché.

"Okay," Dad said. "Let's get this show on the road."

Rocket grabbed his new stick and we piled into the car. One of our neighbors, Mr. Hammann, was outside his house and he shouted, "Go get 'em, Dusk!"

A big sign in front of the Molson Centre said TONIGHT: THE MILLION DOLLAR GOAL! We pulled into a special V.I.P. parking space. Even though we were early, the lot was already beginning to fill up.

That Miss Dunn lady met us and told us there was somebody she wanted us to meet. She led us through a bunch of tunnels under the stadium and opened a door that said JANITOR on it.

We walked in and there were a bunch of guys sitting on benches. It took about a second for us to realize they were not janitors. They were the Montreal Canadiens! We were in the Canadiens locker room! Pierre Lapointe, Lars Nilsson, and Ivan Turgeon were sitting there in the flesh! Well, they had clothes on, I mean. But they were there. Our heroes were right in front of us.

The players looked up at us standing in the doorway, and they must have recognized Rocket from pictures in the paper or something because one by one they all stood up and started clapping. It was real embarrassing.

It was embarrassing for Dawn. For me, it was like a dream come true.

They all gathered around us and started saying they were sorry to hear about Oma and wishing Rocket good luck. They all signed Rocket's stick and gave me autographed pictures. It was awesome.

"The crucial thing, kid," said Lars Nilsson, throwing his arm around Rocket, "is to forget about the crowd, forget about the noise, forget about the world. Reduce everything down to you, the stick, the puck, and that beautiful million dollar check."

By the time we got out of the locker room and over to the private box that had been reserved for us, most of the seats in the Molson Centre were filled. Lots of people were wearing Dad's yellow T-shirts. Some of them were holding signs that said BLEEP BLEEP! on them. Rocket started to put on his skates, but we all told him he was being ridiculous. He wouldn't be shooting for the million dollar goal until after the Canadiens game was over.

The game was one big blur to me. We had great seats, but I didn't see much. I sat there watching every second of it, but I barely remember what happened. The Canadiens won, I think.

My mind was on the shot. I was rehearsing over and over again in my head exactly how I was going to shoot it. Somebody had told me that great athletes visualize succeeding in their minds before a competition, and it helps them succeed. That's what I was trying to do.

Yes, the Canadiens won, 3–2. It was a great game. Ivan Turgeon scored the winning goal with less than a minute left. It's hard to believe Rocket doesn't remember it.

"You can lace up those skates now, son," Dad said as the Canadiens congratulated each other. "It's showtime."

We gave Rocket one last hug for luck as the intro to "Blue Suede Shoes" blared out of the speakers.

The people who were heading for the exits turned around and went back to their seats. A guy wearing a referee's uniform (I'm not sure if he was a real ref or not) came to our box to get Rocket. Dad got out his video camera and started shooting.

At one end of the rink, some workers had already taken away the regular goal, and they were replacing it with a big wooden semicircle that had a rainbow painted on it. At one end of the rainbow—instead of a pot of gold—was a neon-yellow check. I looked through Dad's binoculars to see if I could make out the writing on it, but it was too far away.

"Who wants to see us give away some money?" boomed the "ref" into a handheld mike.

"Yeeeeeeeaaaaaaaaaahhhhhhhhhhhh!"

When Rocket stepped out on the ice, a huge roar erupted from the stands. He looked nervous to me. If he hadn't been nervous, he would have been bowing and waving and clowning for the fans.

Of course I was nervous! What else would I be? There were more than 20,000 people staring at me, not to mention the millions of people who were watching on TV. I really had to pick my nose, but I knew it would be a terrible time to do that.

"Ladies and gentlemen, approaching center ice is Dusk Rosenberg, who will be attempting to shoot a million dollar goal! Let's make some noise for him!"

He didn't have to encourage the crowd. They were already chanting "Dusk! Dusk! Dusk!"

See? If I'd had my nickname then, they would have been chanting "Rocket! Rocket! Rocket!"

"Before Dusk takes his shot," the announcer said, "please rise and remove your hats. We would like to have a moment of silence in honor of Dusk's grandmother, our beloved Sophie Rosenberg, who as you know could not be with us this evening."

It was totally quiet in the Molson Centre, except for scattered sobbing I could hear around us. The moment of silence was broken by music from the sound system. It was Elvis, singing "Love Me Tender."

It's not one of his rock-and-roll songs. It's really slow and quiet. I had heard the song before, but I never really listened to the words. They are really beautiful.

By the time "Love Me Tender" was over, Mom and Dad and I were pretty choked up. Across the stadium, I could hear people weeping, wailing, and sniffling into handkerchiefs.

The folks who were running the contest must have felt it was too depressing, because as soon as "Love Me Tender" was over, they switched to "All Shook Up," and the joint was rocking again.

"Win it for Granny!" somebody hollered.

"Straight and true, Dusk!"

"You can do it, kid!"

They put Rocket's picture up on the JumboTron screen so his face was about ten feet high. He looked a little scared, but determined too. I was glad it wasn't me out there. I'm not sure I would have been able to handle the pressure.

They showed the check up on the screen too. Now I could make out the writing: PAY TO THE ORDER OF DUSK AND DAWN ROSENBERG. ONE MILLION DOLLARS AND NO CENTS.

"The rules are simple," announced the referee. "If Dusk can knock over the check with the puck, he gets to keep it. The check that is, not the puck. If he misses, he will get a year's supply of Pirelli's delicious pizza, courtesy of our newest sponsor. Any way you slice it, Pirelli Pizza is the nicest."

Dad glanced up from his video camera for a moment to throw Mom and me a grin. "Catchy slogan," he said.

"Dusk! Dusk! Dusk!"

The ref took a puck from his pocket. It was gold. While he was holding it up to show the crowd, a woman came out on the ice pushing an empty wheelchair. She parked it next to Rocket.

"I think it's really nice to see that they're honoring Oma this way," Mom said, wiping her eyes with a tissue.

They didn't bring out the wheelchair to honor Oma. The lady who brought out the chair said to me, "Have a seat," and I said, "What for?" and she said, "Because you're supposed to sit here," and I said, "Says who?" and she said, "That's the arrangement," and I said, "Since when?" and she said—

Oh, let me tell it. It wasn't until later that we got the full explanation. After the first time Oma went to the hospital and was told she shouldn't walk anymore, we wanted to make sure she would be allowed to use a wheelchair to shoot the million dollar goal. The Canadiens said that would be fine, and they even put it in the contract that "the contestant" would be sitting in a wheelchair. But now, the contestant was Rocket.

In other words, Rocket would have to take the shot under the exact same conditions Oma would have taken the shot—sitting in a wheelchair.

Well, you should have seen Dad! He handed Mom the video camera and bolted out of his seat, running on the ice and screaming it was unfair, the Canadiens were a bunch of crooks, that he was going to call his lawyer, and so on.

The crowd had a good laugh when Dad slipped on the ice and fell on his behind. But when they realized that Rocket was being told to sit in the wheelchair, they started booing, shouting rude things, and throwing stuff on the ice. Some security police came out, crossing their arms in front of them and looking menacing. It was getting ugly out there.

I realized I'd better do something or the crowd might get out of control. So I asked the referee guy if I could use the microphone, and he gave it to me.

"Listen up, everybody!" Rocket said. "My grandmother, Sophie Rosenberg, may she rest in peace, used to enter every contest she saw. Oma used to sit at our kitchen table for hours filling out contest applications. And she always told me, 'You've got to play by the bleeping rules. If you don't play by the bleeping rules, you can't bleeping win.' So in honor of Oma, I am going to play by the rules as they are written."

With that, Rocket sat in the wheelchair, and the crowd roared in approval. What a class act! I have never been so proud of my brother in my life.

Dad returned to his seat, and we brushed the ice off his pants. The ref took the microphone back and handed Rocket a sawed-off hockey stick, which had been in a bag hanging off the back of the wheelchair.

"Dusk! Dusk! Dusk!" the crowd began chanting.

Some of the Canadiens must have heard the commotion from their locker room, because they came out on the ice to watch.

The ref placed the puck on the red line, in the middle of the face-off circle. Rocket maneuvered the wheelchair around until it was about a foot to the left of the puck. He swung his arm around a few times to loosen up his muscles.

"Dusk! Dusk! Dusk!"

The ref told me to take my time, but with each passing second I was getting more tense. The crowd was so loud, it sounded like the vibration from their yelling, clapping, and stomping might make the roof cave in. I just wanted to get it over with.

The JumboTron screen kept switching from the image of Rocket's face to the image of the million dollar check. The organist had picked up on the rhythm of the crowd chanting, and she was pounding out chords to go with it. Dad was shooting video. Mom was praying.

Forget about the crowd, I told myself. Forget about the noise. Forget about the world. All that mattered was me, the stick, the puck, and that beautiful million dollar check down there.

Rocket leaned over the side of the wheelchair

and put the blade of the short stick on the ice right behind the puck. Then he looked down the ice at the little target. He narrowed his eyes slightly, taking aim, and took a deep breath.

And then he took his shot.

ANY DAY NOW

There are only two possible ways this story could end. . . .

1. Rocket could make the shot. Everybody would scream and we'd run out on the ice. Dad would fall down again. We'd all live happily ever after, and a million dollars richer.

2. Rocket could miss the shot to the left or right. Twenty thousand people would let out a collective sigh. Rocket and I would go back to being plain old normal kids again, except we would have all the pizza we could ever eat.

That is so totally wrong it's not even funny.

Don't you have any imagination? There are lots of other possible ways the story could have ended.

3. The moment I hit the puck, an electrical storm causes all the power to go out in the Molson Centre. The lights go out. When they go back on, the puck is gone. The check is gone. Nobody knows where it is, or whether the puck hit it or not.
4. The moment I hit the puck, Sheldon Silverman (who had recently escaped from jail) dashes past security, runs on the ice, and throws himself in front of the puck in a desperate attempt to prevent me from winning the million dollars.
5. Oma isn't dead at all. She has faked her own death. At the last possible instant, she comes out on the ice and shoots the million dollar goal herself.
6. The moment I hit the puck, a dog comes running out on the ice and grabs the puck in its mouth and runs away with it. We never know if my shot would have hit the target or not.

7. It was all a dream. None of this even happened.

Are you finished? Because this is really ridiculous.

No, I'm not. How about this one? The moment I hit the puck, an alien spaceship crashes through the roof of the Molson Centre—

Are you finished?

No.

Please excuse my brother. I'm afraid that in all the excitement over the million dollar goal, something happened to his brain.

In any case, this is what really happened. . . .

Rocket took the shot.

The puck was sliding across the ice.

I held my breath.

It looked like the puck was sliding in slow motion, somehow.

It looked like it was straight and true, but it was hard to tell from where we were sitting.

As the puck got closer to the check, I could tell it was going to be close.

So could the rest of the crowd. A slow roar built up with every foot of ice the puck crossed.

When it was about ten feet away, it looked like

the shot was going to be on the money, so to speak.

When it was five feet from the check, I had to cover my ears because the people behind us were shrieking so loud I thought my eardrums were going to explode.

Two feet from the check, we were out of our seats, jumping from the sheer exhilaration of the experience.

And then . . .

19

DON'T CRY DADDY

The puck stopped. One bleeping inch from the check, it ran out of gas and stopped, like a bug that had been stepped on.

Oh, stop your boo-hooing.

We lost. That's right, Rocket missed the shot. I repeat, *missed*. Do not pass GO, do not collect a million dollars.

Couldn't you just say that I made the shot? That would make a much better ending to the story.

You missed. Deal with it, okay? Life isn't a bowl of cherries, as our dad likes to say. Sometimes we fail. Sometimes we lose. Sometimes the hero doesn't get the girl. Sometimes the bad guy wins. We don't always live happily ever after and walk off into the sunset holding hands. Sometimes there's no happy ending. That's life.

Rocket hit it perfectly, but he just didn't quite hit it hard enough. The puck just sat there on the ice an inch from the check, like it was waiting for a traffic light to turn green. The crowd gasped. Rocket tumbled out of the wheelchair and dropped to his knees, his forehead touching the ice. He pounded a fist against the ice. It was all over.

In the movie version, I'll hit the check, okay? Why do they always do that? You read a perfectly good, depressing story, and then they change it around to give it some dumb happy ending. I hate that.

Are you finished?

No.

20

GOOD LUCK CHARM

Every time he thinks he's been wronged, Dad always says he's going to call his lawyer. But he never actually did it. I had never met dad's lawyer. To tell you the truth, I didn't even believe Dad really had a lawyer.

But there we were, sitting in the law offices of Eric Gullikson, Esq. I don't know what Esq. means, but that's what lawyers call themselves for some reason. Eric Gullikson was an old, gray guy who looked like he had no sense of humor at all.

"Let me first offer my deepest regrets on the passing of your loving mother Sophie," the lawyer said to Dad after we had settled into the thick couches in his office. Blah-blah-blah. After some small talk (which grown-ups always seem to have to do before they say what they came to say), we got down to the business of going over Oma's will.

A will is short for Last Will and Testament. It's basically a contract that grown-ups write up that says who gets their stuff after they're dead. If somebody dies and they don't have a will, the living relatives have to fight it out, I guess, to decide who gets what. The whole thing is kind of creepy, but it's just one of those unpleasant things that comes with being an adult, like having to trim the hair that grows out your ears (which my dad does every week, and it's disgusting).

Oma didn't have a lot of money or a lot of stuff. If she did, she probably wouldn't have been living with us all those years. She had a few thousand dollars in a savings account, which she left to Dad. I knew it didn't even cover the cost of her funeral. Most of her possessions weren't worth anything, but she did leave her jewelry to Mom. A lot of her stuff we would just have to sell or donate to charity.

"'. . . and to my grandchildren, Dawn and Dusk Rosenberg,'" the lawyer read from the will, "'I leave my framed portrait of Elvis Presley (which he gave me personally) in hopes that they might someday appreciate the King the way that I did.'"

It was a serious occasion and all, but we had to laugh. The lawyer took the Elvis portrait out of his closet and handed it to us.

"Velvet Elvis!" I guffawed. "She left us Velvet Elvis?"

"Now we're stuck with it for the rest of our lives!" Rocket moaned.

Even Mom and Dad thought it was funny that Oma had given us Velvet Elvis, probably because they would finally be getting rid of it themselves.

"Hey!" Rocket said, snapping his fingers, "Maybe that's what Oma meant when she said 'Elvis lives.' Those were her last words, remember? Elvis lives. Now that we've got this stupid portrait, Elvis will always live with us."

"Whether we like it or not," I added.

The four of us were discussing Velvet Elvis and having a laugh over it when the lawyer cleared his throat.

"I don't think that's what your grandmother meant when she said 'Elvis lives.'"

We all looked at him.

"I took the liberty of examining this piece of 'art'

thoroughly before giving it to you," he said, putting on a pair of white gloves he'd pulled from his desk drawer. "One never knows what one might find in these situations."

"Did you find something?" Mom asked.

"I removed the thick cardboard backing," he said, as he took the picture out of the frame, "and lo and behold, this document fell out."

He handed a piece of paper to Rocket very carefully. I leaned over to read it over his shoulder.

"It's some sort of a contract," Rocket said.

"A birth certificate," the lawyer corrected him.

"It's Elvis Presley's birth certificate!" I shouted. The name *Elvis Aron Presley* was right there on the top line. The date of birth was January 8, 1935. It was *real*!

"Are you sure?" Mom asked, and we all gathered around to look at the paper.

"Why would he hide his birth certificate in the back of a portrait?" Dad wondered.

"Is it a one of a kind?" I asked.

"This could be worth a lot of money!" Rocket said.

"I can't answer all your questions," the lawyer told us. "I don't know what would possess someone to hide their birth certificate behind a painting. Perhaps Mr. Presley didn't even know it was there when he gave it to your grandmother. But I do know that it is original, it is authentic, and one of a kind. I had a Presley memorabilia expert look it over, and he appraised it in the neighborhood of one million dollars."

None of us said anything for what felt like an hour but was probably five seconds. Then we all started talking at once.

"A million dollars?" Dad asked. "Are you *sure*?"

"Oma was a millionaire!" Mom exclaimed.

"So *that's* what she meant by 'Elvis lives!'" Rocket said. "She had his birth certificate, the written legal proof that he was born!"

"Oh, stop it," I told him. "We don't even know if Oma knew the birth certificate was there."

"Who cares what she meant by 'Elvis lives'?" Rocket insisted. "Long live the King of Rock and Roll! Wop-bop-a-loom-a-boom-bam-boom!"

Well, that's the story, pretty much the way it happened.

I guess it did have a happy ending after all.

Yeah, I guess so.

So in other words, life *is* a bowl of cherries. Sometimes we win. Sometimes we live happily ever after and walk off into the sunset. Sometimes you get to dance in the end zone, even if there is no end zone. Sometimes—

Are you finished?

Yes.